Blackout

&

Other Stories

J.T. McDaniel

Blackout and *Survivor* were originally published in the *Riverdale Short Story Annual 2005*, © 2005, Riverdale Electronic Books, Riverdale, Georgia.

Mort's Maid, Predator, A Patient Man, and *Castle Grosshelm* were originally published on JacobThomson.com, © 2004, "Jacob Thomson."

Skagerrak was originally published on JTMcDaniel.com, © 2001, J.T. McDaniel.

Memoir was originally published in the *Riverdale Vampire Collection*, Riverdale Electronic Books, Inc., Cumming, Georgia. © 2009, J.T. McDaniel.

Blackout, Survivor, Mort's Maid, Predator, A Patient Man, Castle Grosshelm, Skagerrak, and *Memoir* previously appeared in, and *Eighteen Hours* was originally published in, *This and That*, Riverdale Books, Dublin, Ohio, © 2011, J.T. McDaniel.

Digital and audio versions of *Blackout & Other Stories* are published by C.E.B. Pubs, by special arrangement with Riverdale Books, a division of Riverdale Literary Holdings, Inc.

Permissions Department
Riverdale Books, a division of
Riverdale Literary Holdings, Inc.
PO Box 3716
Dublin, OH 43016

Print ISBN: 978-1-932606-41-6
PDF ISBN: 978-1-943288-10-6
ePub ISBN: 978-1-943288-11-3

Published in the United States of America

CONTENTS

INTRODUCTION

Rather obviously, a number of the stories in this book have appeared in other collections. Despite that, you stand a very good chance of finding a good bit of material here that you've never read. I can say that because I've seen the sales figures on the short story collections, and know perfectly well that not that many people ever bought them.

So why am I trying again? Partly, because this time we'll be doing an audio book version, and I'm told that short story collections do a lot better when people listen to them in the car than when they have to sit down and actually read them. As I'll be reading the stories myself, possibly there's an element of curiosity. What does this guy sound like? Which of those accents is the real one?

The largest group of these stories were published as the first section of *This and That*, which also included a section of autobiographical stuff, and an essay collection. Personally, I think I've led a fairly interesting life, but I suppose not everyone thought it was interesting enough to read about it.

Three of the stories, *Element of Surprise*, *The Life of Salmik the Great*, and *Return to Duty*, have never been published before. The first two are the oldest things in this book, written in the middle 1970s, though I've made a few minor changes to them for this collection. *Return to Duty* is actually part of chapter one and most of chapter two of my 1981 novel, *The Highest Honour*. Given the choice, I'd rather publish the entire novel, but all that survived were the first five chapters, so I adapted what was left. It tells a complete story in any case.

Those three stories are set in an ancient civilization I created called the

Gehunite Empire, which I suppose needs a bit of explanation. The Empire was created as a setting for another novel, *Alura*, a long, complex swords and sorcery story about a mercenary princess from a far northern country where the women went to war and the men stayed home and raised the children. If the manuscript hadn't been lost, and I published it today, I'd no doubt hear Xena-clone comments, but they'd be wrong. Lucy Lawless was in grade school when *Alura* was written.

In any case, I set the Gehunite Empire in a period roughly 83,000 years before the start of our present calendar. Long enough ago for an advanced civilization to have developed and disappeared. As to how it disappeared, well, did you know we used to have two moons? The one we still have, and a much smaller one that ended up falling on Atlantis—which is in these stories, but with a different name.

Over a bit more than 800 years, the Gehunite Empire managed to go from a swords and sorcery type mystical culture, to an industrial, scientific culture capable of sending some of its citizens into deep space. If you're wondering how that turned out, I'm working on a novel that should appear sometime in 2016.

The main thing to remember about the Gehunites is that every month on their calendar was 28 days long, the months were called OneMonth, TwoMonth, and so on, and they had 13 of them, plus two holidays that weren't part of any week or month. The days of the week were called First-Day, SecondDay, and so forth, with the usual seven. The Gehunites used a 30 hour clock, with 100 minutes in an hour and 100 seconds in a minute. This means that their hours were shorter than ours. The size of the earth not really having changed that much, measurements are metric, derived the same way. Nautical measurements involved miles, with a nautical mile the same as it is today, one minute of arc measured at the equator, but as the Gehunites defined a circle as 300 degree, with 100 minutes to each degree and 100 seconds to each minute, the actual distance is a bit shorter. Because the clocks and arc were both measured in the same way, this made navigation a good bit simpler, as there was no need to convert between time and arc, as is necessary in our modern system. Other than a couple of odd sounding time and date references in the stories, none of this matters that much, but I thought I'd mention it here anyway.

I mean, really, does anyone actually read these introductions?

BLACKOUT

Jake Holden looked into his glass and wondered, not for the first time that afternoon, just why he was still sitting there. He knew he should be doing something—anything.

Well, he'd already done something, hadn't he? And didn't sitting in a bar with a bourbon and Coke count as doing something, too? He was drinking, which was certainly something.

It just wasn't what he *should* be doing, he thought.

What he *should* be doing was walking four blocks uptown to the bus station, buying a ticket for somewhere else, and getting out of town. They were probably looking for him by now, wanting to talk to him, wanting to ask him what he knew about the two bodies in the master bedroom of his house.

Not that they'd have any real doubts. Any cop who found Irene Holden, naked, in her own bed, with a .45 slug in her head and, right next to her, Harry Custis, also naked and also with a .45 slug in his head, would naturally figure that Jake had something to do with it. Dead naked wife and dead naked neighbor just added up to outraged husband.

Cops thought that way, and you could hardly blame them. It was the way things usually were.

Not this time, though, Jake thought. He had no more idea who had shot Irene and Harry than he did whether Dewey's moustache was really going to be a major issue in the election. His wife thought it would—*had* thought, he corrected himself, since she was dead now and past thinking about anything.

"Another one?" the bartender asked.

"Yeah."

The bartender reached under the bar, grabbing the Old Crow and a bottle of Coca Cola. He filled a clean glass with ice and poured in the bourbon. Then he opened the Coke and filled the glass the rest of the way up, leaving a golden ring of foam floating at the top of the drink. He did it the right way, using a proper 10-ounce glass, which was the only way to get the proportions right. Stingy bartenders used 8-ounce glasses, which saved a couple cents worth of mixer at the cost of something that didn't taste quite the way it should.

"You're awful quiet today," he commented, pushing the drink across the bar.

Jake smiled weakly. "Got a lot to think about, Fred."

"Well, you just go right ahead." The bartender strolled down to the far end of the bar, where he had been talking to a redhead dressed in a white blouse and gray sheath skirt. Jake figured the girl was probably a hooker. Why else would she be in a bar in the middle of the afternoon?

He thought back to when he'd walked into his house a few hours ago, wondering why it smelled of cordite. It had struck him as out of place. It was a smell he associated with the war, when he'd spent a couple years training, and another one killing Germans, not with his own house.

His house was supposed to smell of food cooking, mostly, mixed with the lingering scent of Irene's perfume and his cigars. He smoked big, hand-rolled Cuban coronas, which went with his stocky build and broad face.

He knew both of them were dead as soon as he walked into the bedroom. He'd seen plenty of dead bodies in the war. He knew what they looked like—the way they lay, utterly relaxed, and the pale skin shading to purple in the lower parts.

He hadn't touched anything, which he figured might be something in his own favor. On the other hand, he had also been able to see the serial number on the big Army Colt that lay on the floor beside the bed, and it was his own gun, so even if he hadn't touched it *today*, his fingerprints were probably still on it from any number of other times when he'd handled the thing.

He could only hope that his prints weren't the only ones on the gun, and the killer had been careless enough to leave some evidence as well.

As far as Jake was concerned, the most incriminating evidence would be the two dead bodies in his bed. If you find a wife and a neighbor dead in bed, the natural suspect is going to be the husband.

Or the neighbor's wife? He hadn't thought of that, for some reason. Candace Custis was such a mousy little thing, so completely under her husband's thumb, that it was impossible to think of her as a murderer. It would require too great a sense of self. Jake didn't think Candy had it in her.

But who else was there?

The front door opened, admitting a uniformed police sergeant. All over now, Jake thought. They'll haul me away and I'll wind up in Ossining being cooked for something I didn't do.

The cop just ignored him, walking to the end of the bar. Fred came down to where he was standing—the cop ignored the hooker, too—and pulled a bottle of Coca Cola from under the bar. Knocking off the cap, he dumped about half the Coke into the sink, then topped off the bottle with rum and gave it to the cop.

The cop took the bottle, grinned amiably, and walked out the front door without paying. He'd go back to the station and be able to sit up there behind his desk, looking perfectly innocent, as he sipped at his bottle of soda.

Must be nice, Jake thought. Cops didn't get paid all that much, but they didn't have to pay for booze or food, either, and there was always a little extra to be made if you were willing to ignore a lot of minor crap that probably shouldn't be illegal in the first place.

Like the hooker, for instance. If Harry had been screwing a hooker instead of Irene—Jake was pretty much forced to admit that something had been going on between them, what with finding both of them naked in the same bed—he might not have got himself shot in the head.

Or, if he had, it wouldn't have been with Irene.

Who the hell would want to kill them? Jake wondered. It couldn't be Candy, and he knew damned well that *he* hadn't done it, so who else was there?

It would probably help if he knew when it had happened, he thought. He'd found them when he came home for lunch at 12:15, walking the three blocks from Ferguson's Hardware, where he had been head bookkeeper since getting out of the Army in '46. So it had to be sometime before noon, right?

He had gone to work at 9:30, as usual. He didn't remember the house smelling of gunpowder when he left. He didn't remember two dead bodies in his bed, either.

Yet he really couldn't discount the possibility. He had been right here in this bar until 2:30 in the morning, and Irene tended to be a little irked when he came home drunk, so he'd just taken off his jacket and flopped on the living room couch. He didn't remember going into the bedroom at all.

Hell, he thought, he really didn't remember much of anything about the previous night. Was that significant? You couldn't kill a couple of people, one of them your wife, and be so drunk you didn't remember doing it, could you?

He looked down the bar, to where Fred was still chatting with the red-head. There was something familiar about her, too. He waved to the bartender.

"Yeah?"

"Who's your friend?"

"Who? Kathy?"

3

"Is that her name?"

Fred looked at him curiously. "You telling me you didn't know?"

"Should I?"

"You *did* spend about two hours last night buying her drinks and bending her ear, Jake."

"I did?"

Fred grinned. "And I don't know *what* the two of you were up to in the storeroom."

"In the storeroom?"

"Like I said, I don't know anything. But you both looked pretty happy when you came back out."

Oh, Christ, Jake thought. If I could forget *that*, what else could I forget? Maybe I *did* shoot them.

He took a long swallow of his drink. It didn't burn going down, so his throat must be pretty well anesthetized by now. I drink too damned much, he thought. A little more and I'll start forgetting things again.

Hell, he thought, I've already forgot to go back to work. Ferguson won't be happy about that. Not that it's going to matter very much if I shot my wife. When they stick me in the chair he's going to have to get a new bookkeeper anyway.

He was beginning to realize that he probably *had* killed his wife and her lover. Who else could have done it? It was his gun, his house, and who else had a better motive? More, if he was too drunk to remember what he'd done, the redhead probably *could* recall what they'd done in the storeroom — he wished *he* could — which a jury would take into consideration in ignoring the "unwritten law" argument his lawyer would probably make. A cheating husband would get a lot less slack for killing a cheating wife.

The front door opened again. One of the two men who entered was Ferguson, who pointed his finger at Jake. The other was obviously a detective. For some reason, Jake was pretty sure this one was there for him, and not just stopping off to pick up a flute.

Now what? he thought. It was too late to run, pointless to fight — he was big, but not very strong — and he wasn't smart enough to outwit a detective. Jake had few illusions about himself. Sure, he had been a decent fighter as part of an infantry company, but that was war, and you had everyone else around to support you and, most of the time, you kept the enemy at a distance. One on one was another story.

The detective walked over to him, Ferguson in tow.

"Jacob Holden?"

"Yeah."

"Jake," Ferguson said, "Irene is dead."

Jake blinked. "Huh?"

"Your wife is dead, Mr. Holden," the detective said.

"Uh, yeah. I know."

"How do you know?"

"When I went home for lunch. You could smell the gunpowder, and there they were, the two of them."

The detective nodded. "Right. Your wife and Mr. Custis."

"Right." Jake frowned. "So, now what? Are you going to arrest me?"

"For what?"

Jake shrugged. "Dead wife, dead neighbor, both naked in the same bed. Who else would you suspect?"

"You didn't do it, did you?" the detective asked.

"Not that I know of. I really don't remember much from last night."

"Custis killed your wife, Mr. Holden," the detective said. "Then he killed himself."

"With my gun?"

"He left a note. Said your wife wanted to break it off, and that he couldn't take it, so he was going to kill her and then kill himself."

"With my gun?"

"Where did you keep it?"

"In the nightstand, beside the bed."

The detective nodded. "We found a little H&R .22 in his jacket pocket. His wife identified it as his. I suppose that was what he planned to use, but then he found your gun and probably decided a .45 would be more effective."

Jake picked up his drink and took a long swallow. "I suppose it would be," he said.

"Anyway," the detective went on, "this is the note. Mrs. Custis has identified the handwriting as her husband's."

Jake read the short note several times. There was something about it that didn't seem quite right, but he couldn't place it.

I am going to end it all, the note said. *I cannot live this way, and I cannot live without Irene. We will go on to a better place together. I know some will condemn me for what I am about to do, and I am truly sorry for any pain this will cause, but it is all for the best. I am so sorry, Candy, but you will be better off with someone of stronger moral fibre, and I can only hope you will forgive me. Harry.*

He returned the note to the detective. "I guess that says it all."

"The coroner has the bodies, Mr. Holden. You'll have to go down and make a formal identification, and the law says there has to be an autopsy."

Ferguson put his hand on Jake's shoulder. "Take as much time as you need, Jake," he said. "You'll stay on salary."

"Thanks, Bill." He was still thinking about the note. The formal style was typical of Harry Custis, who was always very careful about his grammar and spelling. But there was something wrong.

"If you're going to be here for a while," the detective said, "I'll send a radio car around to take you down to the morgue."

"Sure. I don't think I'll be going home right away."

"I'll send a car, then."

That was when it hit him. It was a single word in the note, *fibre*, that had started him wondering. Harry Custis *was* pretty obsessive about language. He was also very American, and would admit no authority as higher than Webster. He would have written "fiber."

But Candace Custis was British, a war bride. I never would have believed she'd have it in her, he thought. Still, it wasn't his job to figure these things out. If the detective was any good at his job, he'd notice the British spelling and draw his own conclusions. If he didn't, then she'd get away with it.

It wasn't as if he'd had much of a marriage lately. He'd miss Irene, but he'd get over it. The guilty parties were dead. Was it up to him to mete out punishment to their killer? Or was it one of those cases where sympathy was in order? He'd have to think about that.

He pushed his glass across the bar and signaled for a refill. "I'll be right here," he said.

EIGHTEEN HOURS

U.S.S. *Mako* tugged at the lines securing her to the pier at the Submarine Base, New London, as if eager to get back to the war. It was an illusion, Lieutenant Commander John Billings thought. Eager she might be to return to the Atlantic on her third official war patrol, but it would be stretching things considerably to think of that as getting back to the war.

The war in the Atlantic had been going on since the end of 1939, though the United States had been in it officially for only some 16 months. Out there the convoys fought their way across the Atlantic, or up the coast from the Caribbean to New England. But the only submarines that were doing anything of note belonged to the enemy. *Mako* had made two patrols out of Groton, each time covering an area from the approaches of the Chesapeake Bay up to a line off Cape Cod. On neither of those patrols had *Mako* ever found anything to shoot at.

In the movies American submariners spent their time off the Atlantic coast chasing down German raiders and attacking secret enemy bases, but real life wasn't nearly that exciting. In real life, a patrolling American submarine was more likely to be attacked by a friendly pilot than by an enemy ship. American subs were getting plenty of action in the Pacific, but not around here.

You could hardly expect it to be otherwise, Billings thought. In the Pacific, the submarine war was concentrated on cutting the Japanese supply lines, with the intent not only of stopping them from advancing any farther, but also keeping them from resupplying their earlier conquests. It put the enemy on the defensive, forcing him to allocate valuable resources to protecting his merchant fleet, when they might be better used in support of offensive operations.

It was different in the Atlantic. The German sea lines had been cut long since, though they still tried to slip a ship through the blockade from time to time. German heavy units could no longer operate in the Atlantic with any degree of safety, and it was rumored that Hitler had become so defensive of his few battleships and other heavy fleet units that they were, for all practical purposes, confined to port.

So the ships crossing the Atlantic were nearly all Allied, with a scattering of neutrals. There were no German surface combatants on the western side of the Atlantic. Any American submarines patrolling along the east coast had no targets, with the possible exception of the U-boats that were there to prey on the coastal convoys. Generally, those did their best to keep out of sight.

It was going to be somewhat boring for the next few weeks, Billings thought. Better than training duty at the Submarine School, though. At least on a patrol there was a *chance* of some action.

It had been like this for *Mako* ever since the Japanese attack on Pearl Harbor brought the United States into the war. The third of three *Mackerel* class submarines, and a virtual twin of *Mackerel* herself, *Mako* had been constructed just down the Thames at Electric Boat Company's main yard. The third boat in the class, *Marlin*, had been built at Portsmouth Navy Yard, to a slightly different plan.

The original concept had called for 30 of the *Mackerel* class boats, divided evenly between Groton, Coco Solo in the Panama Canal Zone, and Hawaii. They were smaller than the big fleet type submarines, but somewhat larger, though of less displacement and much more modern, than the S-boats that had made up much of the Asiatic Fleet's submarine force before the Japanese had forced the remnants to retreat to Australia. The boats had been Admiral Hart's idea, intended to be smaller, and thus less expensive, than a fleet boat, but with four tubes forward and two aft, just as heavily armed as the earlier fleet boat classes.

As it turned out, only the three were built, and all of them were now stationed at Groton, making the occasional patrol, but mostly serving as training boats at the Submarine School. Billings' crew was typical, with about two-thirds qualified men and the rest recent graduates who would generally make only a single Atlantic patrol in *Mako* before being sent to the Pacific for assignment. Between patrols, that last third would be made up of students, going to sea for the day as part of their training.

Billings looked at his watch. It was nearly time.

* * *

Dick Rhodes had never expected to find himself in a submarine's control room. After graduating from Sub School, he was sent to San Diego to join a fleet boat deploying to Hawaii, and at that time he had fully expected to be assigned to the engine room. He had been an apprentice locomotive mechanic before enlisting in the Navy the day he received his draft notice. The Army didn't appeal to him, and he figured in the Navy he could at least die clean if it came to that.

When he arrived in San Diego things changed. His boat had left without him, sent off to make a patrol in the Aleutians. Normally, there would be hell to pay for missing a movement, but in this case the boat had departed a week ahead of schedule. Even the Navy didn't punish sailors for failing to show up in the middle of a leave.

So he reported to the base personnel officer. If his ship had gone, the Navy would still want to keep him busy doing something until it got back.

"Do you know anything about GM 16-248 engines, Rhodes?" the personnel officer had asked.

"I've seen them, sir. We got a new switch engine in that had them just before I joined up, but mostly I worked on steam engines."

"Your boat may not be back for two or three months. When she had to sail early we sent another man to fill your slot, so even when she returns there really won't be a place for you."

"I see, sir."

"Now, I can probably find something for you to do here at the base. Or I can put you aboard a tender as relief crew, and at some point you may be assigned to a combat crew. I presume, since you've finished Sub School, you're going to want to get into the fleet and qualify?"

"Naturally, sir."

"But, there's also a slot available at the factory school at the General Motors engine plant in Cleveland. I can send you there for six weeks. Besides learning a lot about those engines, if you finish the course you'll jump to Motor Machinist's Mate Third."

Rhodes hadn't hesitated. If he returned to the railroad after the war the training would be useful. Steam was rapidly being replaced by diesel-electric locomotives, and the chief lure the Navy had held out to Winton and Fairbanks-Morse to develop the lightweight diesels used in fleet submarines was that they would also be highly adaptable to railroad use. Besides, Rhodes had grown up just outside Cleveland, and he would be able to visit his family while he was in school.

It almost certainly meant that he wouldn't be going back to his original boat, even if a place opened up for him later. She'd been a Portsmouth boat, which meant she had Fairbanks-Morse engines. The GM engines—as often as not called "Wintons," after their original builder, who had been bought out by General Motors—went into Electric Boat products.

As it turned out, he went from the General Motors school directly to *Mako*, which, while an Electric Boat product, did *not* have GM engines. Instead, she was equipped with a pair of Electric Boat diesels, which were closer to the GM product than to an F-M, but still sufficiently different that he needed to learn a new design yet again. He spent his first six months in the engine room, doing just that.

And, logically, after he had qualified that was where he should have remained. That had changed one night, about two weeks after he had sewn dolphins onto his jumper sleeve. He had been on the upper deck with Chief Gunner's Mate Reilly, the Chief of the Boat, and two other men. Rhodes had commented on a couple of men standing by a car on the far shore of the Thames and been somewhat surprised when none of the others had seen them.

"Are you sure about that, Rhodes?" Reilly asked.

"Sure."

The COB had squinted into the night, but apparently couldn't make anything out. "Jones," he said, "get up on the bridge and get me a pair of binoculars."

Jones ran back to the fairwater and climbed up to the bridge, returning a moment later with a pair of the 7x50 binoculars the bridge lookouts used at sea. He handed them to Reilly, who put them to his eyes.

"I'll be damned," he said. "There really *are* a couple of guys over there."

No one attached any particular significance to the presence of the two men and a blacked out car on the far shore of the Thames River, since the binoculars revealed them to be cops. But Reilly clearly found the fact that Rhodes could see them unaided significant. He mentioned it to Billings, and the captain quickly changed Rhodes' duty station from the engine room to the control room, where he now handled the bow planes when the boat was submerged, and served as a night bridge lookout when she was on the surface.

"You've got much better than average night vision," Billings had informed him. "So I think you'll be a lot more useful on the bridge than in the engine room."

It didn't matter that much to Rhodes, and he thought it might be interesting to hear what the officers were up to. *Mackerel* class boats were different from the larger fleet boats in their internal arrangements. Instead of the conn and attack party being up in the conning tower, everything was in the control room.

There really was no conning tower in these boats, just a large access trunk where the bridge party could congregate as they surfaced. In a fleet boat, a planesman would only hear what was called down from the conning tower. In *Mako* he got to hear everything.

There were times when Rhodes felt a little guilty, finding himself sitting on his little bench at the bow planes operating wheel instead of back aft, where he could have applied the training the Navy had spent several thousand dollars drilling into him. That guilt passed quickly enough, though, when he took a moment to think about just how damned hot it could get in the engine room, and how much damage the noise back there had no doubt been doing to his ears.

The air conditioning worked a lot better in the control room, and you could generally hear what people were saying without having to resort to lip reading.

When they surfaced at night it was even better. Lookouts got to spend a lot of time up in the fresh air on the bridge.

Three were normally on the same watch, each lookout covering a little more than a third of the circular expanse of ocean surrounding the submarine. Each sector overlapped by a few degrees—no one wanted to take a chance of missing anything between sectors if a lookout didn't turn quite far enough.

The other lookouts on Rhodes' usual watch were Sam Henderson, the BM2c who manned the stern planes, and Caleb Lincoln, an officers' steward. Lincoln once told Rhodes that he figured he had the job because the captain believed the common myth that Negroes had better night vision than whites. Lincoln didn't care very much for the negative aspects of racism—he'd said more than once he would rather be rated as a quartermaster than wait on the officers—but he figured that this particular prejudice was one he could tolerate. At least until winter closed in, and fresh air started to come with frostbite.

Rhodes didn't figure Lincoln's night vision was any better than average. Probably no worse, either. His own, he had to concede, was apparently superior. At least, he often managed to spot things at night that everyone else seemed to miss.

Patrolling in the Atlantic conferred one benefit on the lookouts. Airplanes were somewhat less worrisome than in the Pacific, where just about any plane in the operating area was sure to be Japanese. In the Atlantic you only had friendly planes, even if they were, at times, probably just as dangerous.

"Set the maneuvering watch," the captain ordered, his voice coming over the 1MC.

Rhodes sprang to his feet and hurried up the ladder to the bridge. Throughout the rest of the boat, men hurried to their stations for leaving the pier. They were on their way.

*   *   *

Kapitänleutnant Otto Henschel rested his arms on the bridge coaming, looking over the bow into the moonless night. There was something out there, he thought. There had to be. It was really just a matter of waiting for a target to come along.

It was the waiting that was eating at him. Henschel thought of himself as a patient man, even while he knew that he was lying to himself with such thoughts. He wasn't patient—not where his job was concerned, at least.

U-395 had been on station for two days now, and there had been no traffic worth revealing their presence. Several small fishing boats had passed close by, but Henschel didn't think there was much military value in disrupting the local fishing industry. Not when it would alert the Americans to the presence of a U-boat. He might manage to deny some poor worker his Friday supper, but the reward for that would be that the Americans would divert any worthwhile traffic around his position and flood the area with anti-submarine forces.

There should be tankers, he thought. More than anything else, Dönitz had told his captains to sink tankers. Any enemy merchantman sent to the bottom would help, but tankers would always help a little more. American industry ran on petroleum. The less oil that got through, the less the factories could produce.

Henschel bent over the voice pipe. "Sound room—bridge. Anything yet?"

There was silence for a moment. The sound operator's ears would be covered by his padded headphones, so someone would have to tap him on the shoulder and tell him that the captain wanted a report.

"Bridge—sound room. Very faint HE about 058. Too faint to classify."

"Keep me informed."

It was something, at least, Henschel thought. But it could be anything—even another damned fishing boat.

Things had been easier the first time he came here, Henschel remembered. Not so easy now. Back then the lights had stayed on in the coastal cities and towns, providing a wonderful illuminated backdrop for any passing ships. The silhouetted ships had made easy targets, and American anti-submarine forces had hardly existed.

Now they were learning. The lights were out now, making targets much harder to pick out against the blacked-out shoreline. The anti-submarine forces were still far less effective than their British counterparts, but they were getting better.

But the Americans still hadn't adopted a decent convoy system. He did, at least, have that to be grateful for. The story was that this was because of their Admiral King—the head of the American Navy—or so Henschel had heard. He was apparently an old fashioned sort who believed that small, poorly defended convoys just gave the enemy more concentrated targets, and that they would be more vulnerable than single ships.

Henschel could only hope that he would continue in that particular delusion a while longer.

"Bridge—sound room."

"Bridge, aye."

"HE is becoming clearer, bearing 050, closing. Heavy single screw, reciprocating machinery."

"Range?"

"Still too far to estimate accurately. Perhaps 15 to 20 miles."

Henschel raised his Zeiss binoculars and looked off toward the north. It was a reflexive action, and one he knew would disclose nothing. Whatever was coming this way, it was still too far away to see even had it been daytime.

U-395 was silent now. Earlier, when they had first surfaced after spending the daylight hours resting on the sandy bottom, both engines had been running as they maneuvered into position and charged the batteries. Now, with a full charge, the diesels were shut down, leaving the U-boat to drift silently on station. Henschel knew that sound would normally provide the first indication of an approaching target, and the sound gear worked best when everything aboard that made noise was shut down. It also made it much harder for the enemy to hear *him*.

I still wish I had good radar, he thought. That would be even better.

He kept his binoculars up, scanning the full horizon. As captain, lookout duty wasn't a part of his job, but it was still important that he look around regularly. Each bridge lookout was responsible for his own sector. The captain was responsible for everything. If the patrol was a success it would be Henschel who got the credit. If the patrol was a failure, he would take the blame. Credit, he thought, would be better. Another 12,000 tons would get him his Ritterkreuz.

Even better, it might get him promoted and into a training command. This was his tenth patrol and he had to admit, if only to himself, that he was getting tired. Better to go ashore before he started making mistakes.

"Captain," the port lookout said, "there's something out there at red three-five."

"What is it?"

"Can't quite make it out, sir."

Henschel lifted his binoculars again and focused on the reported bearing. There was something—but what?

"Sound room—bridge. Listen in at about three-two-five. We have visual, but can't make it out."

The report came a minute later, but didn't help much. No engines, no obvious mechanical sounds. The original sound target, however, was getting closer and almost had to be a merchantman of some sort.

Henschel looked again. The image was larger. Quite tall, roughly triangular. Then suddenly it became clear as the approaching vessel changed course slightly, showing more of her profile.

"Schooner," Henschel said. "Looks like a fairly big one."

Big for today, at least, he thought. Three masts, so large enough to be a useful cargo hauler. But also big enough to be useful for other things. There were reports that the Americans were fitting out large sailboats for anti-submarine work. Add a couple guns and some depth charge throwers and you could take advantage of a sailing vessel's inherent silence to sneak up on your prey.

It might even work, he thought. But not this time, if that was what this was.

Still, it presented him with a dilemma. He could certainly sink the schooner with the 88 мм gun on the forward deck. He knew the schooner was there, but it was very unlikely the schooner had spotted *U-395* as yet.

But opening fire with the deck gun would produce a muzzle flash that would be visible for miles on the moonless night. Also, there was a very good chance that if he attacked, the schooner would catch fire. Either was certain to warn the other target, which was probably bigger and thus more valuable. What to do? And what if the schooner really was a sailing Q-ship, or an auxiliary sub chaser? If he couldn't knock out any hidden guns immediately it would take only a single well-placed shell to punch a hole in the pressure hull and leave them unable to dive. After that it wouldn't take long to call up something more powerful to finish the job.

Sinking a sailing ship was supposed to be bad luck. Henschel didn't think of himself as being superstitious, but it would certainly be bad luck to sink a 600 ton schooner if doing so warned away a 10,000 ton tanker.

If that was what the other target was. For all he could say, the distant sound contact might eventually steam into view with a big, illuminated Swedish flag painted on her hull and so be revealed as not a target at all. At least, not one that could be sunk without first boarding her and determining that there was contraband aboard. That was something Henschel could not do this close to an enemy shore, so a neutral would just get a free pass.

Probably not a neutral, though. What to do?

The wind was coming from the starboard beam, which meant the schooner was likely beating to windward on the port tack. At some point she would jibe and head almost directly toward *U-395* as she changed tack.

Maybe, Henschel thought, the best thing would be to just submerge and keep an eye on the schooner until she passed, then come back up and wait for the steamer to come to them. Big targets, he thought, were generally better than small ones.

He lifted his binoculars again, just as the schooner jibed. Now she was sailing almost directly toward him, and in the dark it was hard to judge exactly how far away she was. Not far enough, he decided.

"Clear the bridge."

The lookouts rushed below, followed by *Oberleutnant* Krause, who had been standing his watch with his captain looking over his shoulder. Henschel looked around quickly, then dropped through the hatch, pulling it shut behind him and spinning the locking wheel.

"Dive! Dive! Take her down to thirteen meters."

He took his seat at the conning tower periscope. If it looked as if the schooner was about to collide with them he could go deeper, or simply speed up and get out of the way. Otherwise he would watch her pass.

* * *

Billings lay back in his bunk, glancing down at the gyro repeater and depth gauge mounted above his feet. The captain needed to know what was happening even as he slept—or, at least, tried to sleep.

It was curious, he thought. *Mako* was patrolling about 20 miles east of Long Island, where the chances of finding a real target were close to zero. They had more to worry about from trigger happy Civil Air Patrol pilots than from the enemy, who was probably nowhere around here. The east coast convoy routes were a few miles farther out at this point, and that's where the U-boats would likely be hanging around.

A few more months, he thought, and then it would be over. He would rotate out of *Mako*, probably into new construction, or as a replacement CO on another boat. In all likelihood a fleet boat, and that would mean assignment to the Pacific, where war patrols consisted of more than pointless travel between two fixed points. Out there most of the merchant shipping in the patrol area would be Japanese, making it a legitimate target. With a little luck a captain could rack up a decent score in the Pacific.

In the Atlantic, about all he could rack up was a record of distance steamed.

If there was a good side to all of this, Billings decided, it was that there was no enemy anti-submarine capability to speak of in American coastal waters. Not that you could be complacent—American anti-submarine forces couldn't be entirely relied upon to recognize the difference between a friend and an enemy—but the important thing was that you weren't going to run into a German destroyer off Long Island. In the Pacific operating areas you not only had Japanese merchant shipping to deal with, you also had Japanese escorts, and some of them were evidently pretty good.

Copies of patrol reports went to all American submarine commanding officers, not just the ones in Hawaii and Australia. The comment that, during one depth charge attack, "several of the crew were converted," suggested things had been more than a little tense for that particular boat.

None of that here, though. Planes were a potential problem, but *Mako* was steaming in what was supposed to be a safety zone, and the bridge crew had the proper recognition signals ready, along with standing orders to dive the moment the rockets were fired. That was just in case the pilots didn't see them, or had got the color of the day mixed up, or just didn't care. You couldn't trust aviators, particularly the CAP boys in their light planes. Some rickety little civilian job could ruin you whole day if he managed to drop a bomb onto your bridge.

Billings actually felt a little guilty about taking a nap, though he knew he needed the sleep. Captains didn't stand watches, but had to be available during all of them. With *Mako* on the surface, in broad daylight, he felt that he should be on the bridge, not in his bunk. But he had a competent OOD on duty, and the daylight was, strangely, the safest time to be surfaced in these waters. The U-boats were mostly night hunters—right now they'd be sitting on the bottom, waiting for dark, with most of the crew asleep.

*   *   *

Henschel sat at his narrow desk, pen in hand, carefully writing up his personal journal. You weren't supposed to keep such things at sea, but he doubted that he was unique in defying that particular rule. He was certain several of the enlisted men were also jotting down their daily observations, much to the annoyance of the security people, who saw everything as a possible aid to the enemy.

The official log, the *Kriegstagebuch*, was completed daily and would be turned in to BdU upon return to port. Personal journals and diaries would go home with their creators, and so were not as secure from prying eyes. So the security people reasoned, at least. Henschel was quite sure that his wife wouldn't be reading his journal and, even if she did, he couldn't imagine she'd immediately transmit the contents to enemy intelligence. She'd probably just get nervous about his chances of coming home from the next patrol.

She was nervous about that in any case, he was sure. That would be another reason to get himself into a shore job. He could go home at night, where she could see him and not have to worry so much.

He felt his head nodding. He would need to climb into his berth very soon, where he would sleep, probably right up against the pressure hull, as the boat was now settled on the bottom with about a six degree list to port.

But he needed to finish writing first. He hoped that the previous night had been a turning point in the patrol.

U-395 had remained at periscope depth, watching the schooner pass some 200 meters abeam before again changing tack and opening the angle as she sailed away. It would have been a shame to destroy her, Henschel thought. There was a particular beauty in sailing vessels that you rarely found in more modern commercial vessels. It was as if the designers had kept their esthetic senses turned on in the old days, but let them atrophy once steam came to dominate the seas. Some of the big liners were beautiful ships, but the ordinary freighters and tankers were strictly utilitarian.

He had waited another 20 minutes after the schooner was lost from sight of the more sensitive night periscope in the control room, then brought *U-395* back to the surface. The sound contact had continued to draw closer. On a moonless night, Henschel would want to make a surface attack, using the bridge sight. The slender attack periscope was useless beyond a few hundred meters in such darkness, and the night periscope wasn't that much better.

The bridge sight, incorporating powerful binocular optics, would give a much clearer sight picture. The boat would also be better placed to take evasive action, should the target decide to shoot back. Most merchant ships now mounted at least one deck gun, usually with a Navy crew to man it. And should they call up a destroyer, the best defense was really to be somewhere else by the time it arrived. You could do that easier at 18 knots on the surface than at the three or four knot speed dictated by the need to conserve the batteries when submerged. They were more maneuverable on the surface as well.

It was simply the nature of a submarine. They were surface warships, really, that had been given a limited ability to submerge in order to attack, or to evade the inevitable counter attack. No one had given that much thought to high speed performance while submerged since the earliest days. The first Holland boats had been somewhat faster submerged than modern submarines, but they had been miserable sea boats on the surface, and unless someone came up with something better than batteries for submerged power it was surface performance that mattered most when getting from one place to another.

So they had surfaced and resumed the hunt.

By that time König had replaced Krause as Officer of the Watch. König was *U-395*'s navigating officer, actually an *Obersteurmann*, a chief petty officer, rather than a commissioned officer. *U-395* carried only four commissioned officers. *Oberleutnant zur See* Hermann Krause was the *Erster Wachsoffizier*, or IWO — the Executive Officer, as the Americans would say. The *Zweiter Wachsoffizier*, the IIWO, was *Leutnant zur See* Karl von Holst, and was, in Henschel's opinion, rather more full of himself than even his aristocratic ancestry could ever hope to justify.

The fourth commissioned officer was *Kapitänleutnant (ing)* Wilhelm Rosenberg, the *Leitender Ingenieur*, who was usually called "LI" in conversation. In addition to having charge of the engineering department, he was also the dive officer. Nominally senior to Henschel by two years, Rosenberg's choice of the engineering branch meant that he would be forever subordinate to whatever line officer commanded the vessel he served in, regardless of rank or seniority. Engineers could not hold a command at sea, nor would most have wanted to.

Rosenberg might know everything there was to know about M.A.N. and Maybach diesel engines, but he couldn't navigate his way across the Wannsee, much less the Atlantic.

The ship had come into view about two hours after the schooner had sailed over the horizon.

"Ship, bearing green five-five," the starboard lookout reported.

König and Henschel both trained their binoculars on the indicated bearing. "Got her, sir," König said.

Henschel was straining his eyes. "Can't quite make her out yet," he said, "but I don't see any navigation or hull lights, and that makes her a target."

A neutral would have been burning her navigation lights, as well as having a national flag painted on her sides, which would be brightly illuminated at night. The only other off limits vessels were hospital ships, and they were always painted white and had a big red cross painted on the side. Like neutrals, they burned their navigation lights, illuminated their hulls, and steered a straight course.

"Let's start the approach," Henschel said. He bent over the voice pipe. "Control room — bridge."

"Control room, aye."

"Pass the word. Crew to battle stations, torpedo. Surface action."

"Ship closed up at battle stations, torpedo," came the report, less than a minute later. The boat had been waiting for the target to come to her long enough. Most of the off watch crew had probably been at their battle stations already.

"Bridge—sound room. Target bearing zero-five-two, estimate 14 knots."

"Shouldn't be too long," Henschel mused. He was letting the target come to him, U-395 making bare steerage way on the choppy sea. With no moon there was only a slight chance that a lookout on the target would pick out their wake. Still, it seemed foolish to take even that small chance when there was no real need to chase down the target. In a few minutes the target would likely steam right across his bow. He just needed to be in the right position when it happened.

"Keep a sharp lookout and mind your sectors," Henschel said. There was always a risk at this point in the approach. As the target came into sight it was natural for everyone on the bridge to want to watch. It was a temptation that had to be resisted. Just because there was a target ahead didn't mean someone else wasn't sneaking up on you from another quarter.

"Sound room—bridge. Range to target?"

The sound operator would key the active sonar, sending a single ultrasonic ping to reflect off the target's hull. It was the most accurate way to get a range, and unless the ship had sonar the ping against the hull was unlikely to be heard. Accommodations in a merchantman would all be above the waterline. The only men low enough in the hull to hear the ping would be in the engine room, where it would likely be too noisy to hear anything.

"Bridge—sound room. Range to target three-two-eight-five, bearing zero-four-three."

"Increase to five knots," Henschel ordered. It was time to close the range a bit.

* * *

Henschel bent over the bridge sight a final time. The target's bow was just entering the field of view. Only a few seconds more, he thought. He had the attack calculated nicely. The first torpedo would be fired as the bow crossed the vertical wire in the sight, the second as the back of the forward superstructure did the same. With a run of 950 meters, that should insure that the first "eel" struck about a third of the way along the hull and the second about 15 meters further aft.

The torpedoes were set to run straight. It was a simple matter of geometry. The bridge sight was locked at a preset angle of seven degrees. You didn't fire torpedoes at the target, you fired them at where the target would be at the time they reached its track. With the target crossing the bow at a 90° angle about the only thing that could go wrong was if someone on the target spotted the U-boat and managed to change course quickly enough to avoid the torpedoes.

There was only a slight chance of being spotted, Henschel thought, and even less of the target being able to get out of the way in time.

Another second or two, he thought. "Number One—fire!"

The boat shuddered slightly as the first torpedo was thrust from the tube, the water seeming to bulge upward along the starboard bow. The electric torpedo would swim silently toward the target after diving to a depth of four meters. The G7e ran at 30 knots, slower than the 40 knot G7a, but the electric motor didn't leave the visible wake of the faster wet heater "eel."

"Number Two—fire!"

No one spoke on the bridge. In the conning tower Krause would be timing the torpedo runs with a stopwatch, watching the dim shape of the target in the attack periscope.

The first hit just abaft the forward superstructure. If the second torpedo hit, Henschel was unable to tell. One moment the low riding profile of a laden tanker was crossing his bow and an instant later the entire horizon had vanished in a roiling ball of flame rising furiously into the sky.

"Down!" Henschel shouted. "Behind the bulwark!"

He immediately followed his own advice as a wave of heated air rolled outward from the explosion and across the U-boat. Shards of metal clattered off the superstructure, a jagged piece of hull plating coming over the bulwark and banging off the forward periscope housing. It was about ten centimeters wide, and perhaps twice that in length, shaped something like an arrowhead.

"That could have hurt," König said.

It appeared that nothing more was going to come crashing down, so Henschel stood again to survey the scene. "I think that we may safely classify the target as a gasoline tanker," he said.

"No survivors, I suppose, sir?" König asked.

"Not after that." Henschel looked down at the gyro repeater. "Time for us to get out of here, I think." He bent over the voice pipe. "Control—Bridge. Come left to new course two-six-eight, revolutions for fifteen knots."

That explosion would have been visible for miles, probably even ashore. Someone was sure to come out to investigate and Henschel wanted to be miles away when they arrived.

*   *   *

"Bridge—radar."

Billings toggled the talk switch on the 7MC. "Bridge, aye."

"Contact, bearing three-one-niner, range eight-oh-double-oh."

"Course and speed?"

"Contact appears stationary."

Billings looked over at the OOD. "Thoughts, Mr. Fuller?"

"I think we might want to investigate, sir. If there's something out there that isn't moving, it might just be interesting."

"Excellent idea. Get us over there."

"Aye, aye, sir." Fuller glanced at the gyro repeater. *Mako* was steaming on a heading of 165, near the southern limit of her patrol area.

"Helm—bridge."

"Helm, aye."

"Come left to new course one-two-four. Ahead two thirds."

"Come left to one-two-four," the helmsman repeated. "Ahead two thirds."

Fuller and Billings watched the gyro repeater tick around and steady on the new course. Edwards was on the helm. A first class quartermaster, there would be no question of him overshooting the new course.

"Bridge — helm. Steady on one-two-four, ahead two thirds."

"What would you expect to find?" Billings asked. This was officially a war patrol, but in these waters that still meant it would predominantly be training. Fuller had been promoted to lieutenant (junior grade) less than a month ago, and had pinned a set of gold dolphins to his uniform just before *Mako* set out on her current patrol. He was qualified, but barely, and like any junior officer still had a lot to learn.

"I'm hoping for a U-boat," he said, "but I don't suppose that's really all that likely. Could be someone in trouble, though."

"We're in a pretty good area to find a Kraut lurking about," Billings said. "We lost a big gasoline tanker last night, about 50 miles south of here. Whoever got her wouldn't hang around there, but he *could* turn up around here."

"You think it's a U-boat, sir?"

"We will presume it is, Mr. Fuller. Until we know different. Basic rule — always presume that a contact is something that might want to take a shot at you."

Very sensible, Fuller thought.

*   *   *

"Bridge — sound room. Faint HE, somewhere astern." The hydrophone array was built into the forward edges of the bow plane guards. An accurate angle of bearing was possible for targets bearing between about 275° and 85°, but very iffy for anything farther aft.

Henschel bent over the voice pipe. "Helm — Bridge."

"Helm, aye."

"I want to swing the boat around onto a reciprocal bearing. Go ahead slow port, astern slow starboard. Ten degrees right rudder." He took a quick glance at the compass. "Make your heading about three-double-oh."

The combination of the rudder with the starboard screw trying to pull the boat astern while the port screw tried to push her forward would swing the boat with only a minimum of forward motion. The new heading should give the sound man a much better idea of what they might be dealing with.

Slowly *U-395* began to swing to starboard. The batteries were fully charged and he was using only the electric motors for the maneuver. It would use up some of the charge, but it would be silent. Henschel disliked the idea of making noise. His sole exception was the noise of his torpedoes blasting the bottom out of a target. When you did that, you had to expect noise. But otherwise he would remain as quiet, and as unobtrusive, as possible.

After a little over a minute the compass was indicating a heading of

298°, which would do nicely. It clearly seemed to please the sound man. "HE at green oh-one-oh," he reported. "Twin screws, diesel machinery, making turns for about twelve knots."

"Range?"

"Estimate about three thousand meters, closing."

Henschel trained his binoculars on the indicated bearing, but could see nothing on the moonless night. Still, the sound report was probably enough. Most merchantmen had single screws. Two screws could mean a large, high speed freighter, or a small passenger ship, but both of those would have steam machinery, not diesel. That meant it was most likely another submarine, and there shouldn't be any other U-boats within about 60 miles in either direction.

"I think we may have company," he told Krause.

"American patrol boat, you think?"

"Or an American submarine. In either case, I think perhaps we should submerge before he gets here. I want there to be only one target tonight."

"Krause nodded. "What if he's a destroyer?"

"Two screws and diesel machinery? Unlikely. In any case, we know he's coming this way, so we can prepare a proper welcome, eh?" He looked aft. "Clear the bridge." Then, bending over the voice pipe, "No alarm, pass the word. Dive! Dive!"

*   *   *

"Conn—radar. Target is fading."

"What do you make of it?" Billings demanded.

"Probably a U-boat submerging. The return isn't getting weaker, more like smaller."

"Maneuvering—conn. Shut down the engines, all ahead one third on motors."

"Maneuvering, aye. Shut down engines, all ahead one third on motors."

Back in the engine room the motor machinist's mates on duty shut off the fuel supply to the big diesel engines, and in a moment they grumbled and clattered into silence.

"Sonar—conn. Listen at about three-six-zero."

There was silence for nearly a minute, then, "Conn—sonar. Submarine, dead ahead, range about two-eight-double-oh, submerging. I can hear her tanks venting clear as you'd ever want."

"Do you think that means he's spotted us, Captain?" Fuller asked.

"I'm going to have to figure he has. Which means we need to get under water quick, before we get too close." Billings looked across the bridge at the OOD. "Which means now, Mr. Fuller."

"Aye, aye, sir." Fuller turned momentarily, shouted, "Clear the bridge!" worked the diving alarm switch twice, and switched on the 1MC microphone. "Dive! Dive!"

The boat was already starting under as Fuller, the last man down, pulled the hatch shut and kept tension on the lanyard as the quartermaster of the watch climbed partway up the ladder and spun the locking wheel. The hatch secure, Fuller dropped down the interior ladder to the control room.

"Level off at 100 feet," Billings ordered. "Maintain course."

Lieutenant Norris, the XO, was in the control room now. "Now what, Captain?" he asked.

"Now we try to stay close and wait for him to surface," Billings said. "He can't shoot at us while we're submerged, but we can't shoot at him, either. So we stick close, wait until he comes up for air, and put a torpedo into him."

Norris nodded slowly. "Do you suppose he has the same idea?"

"I wouldn't doubt it. But I don't see an alternative. If this was out in the Pacific I suppose I'd try to sneak away. Plenty of other targets to shoot at there. But this U-boat is probably the only target we'll find in this war. That makes me want to sink him." He looked around the control room. "Besides, the odds are pretty good this is the bastard that blew up that tanker last night. If he's still around, that means he still has torpedoes, and we can't have him doing that sort of thing in our patrol area, can we?"

It was clearly a rhetorical question, Norris and Fuller both recognized.

"There is one thing to consider, Captain," Norris commented, as the two of them bent over the chart table.

"What's that?"

"What if he can hold his breath longer than we can?"

Billings raised an eyebrow. It was, he decided, a valid question. In a fleet boat no one would have raised it. A fleet boat's significantly larger pressure hull meant more air inside and several hours longer submerged before the air started to run out.

"It would be nice to know what we're dealing with," Billings said. "If he's a Type VII boat, that means he's about the same size and should have to come up about the same time. If he's one of their big Type IX boats he probably has four or five more hours of air than we do."

"So what do we do, Captain?"

"We wait. The Krauts have a lot more of the Type VIIs than Type IXs, so the odds are in our favor. Put out the smoking lamp, and anyone who isn't on duty go lay down and try not to breath any more than necessary. It's going to be a waiting game."

*　　*　　*

Henschel had come to the same conclusion, but was taking a different direction. He concluded that, while it would be nice to sink an American submarine, doing so would contribute less to the war effort than getting another merchantman. It would also put his own boat at unnecessary risk.

"What do you suppose an American submarine is doing around here?" Krause asked.

"Probably in transit," Henschel said. "They build the things in Connecticut and Maine. After that, they have to sail them south along the coast, down to Panama, and across the Pacific to where they can annoy our little yellow allies."

"You don't care for the Japanese, Captain?"

"They build good ships, but they don't seem to know how to use them properly. I spoke to a Japanese submarine officer once in Berlin. He told me that it was better to go after warships, and that merchantmen were always secondary targets. It seemed to be a matter of honor; it was better to fight an equal than to attack an inferior."

"Nothing wrong with honor," Krause said. "But warships can't carry much cargo, and infantry need that cargo to continue to fight. Destroy their supply lines and eventually they run out of bullets and have to give up. Sink enough tankers and the warships are out of it anyway for lack of fuel."

"Exactly. We understand this. So do the Americans, from all I've heard. I wouldn't ignore a battleship or aircraft carrier if one happened to cross my sights, but convoy escorts have little strategic value compared to a big freighter full of tanks, or a liner carrying an infantry division."

Krause looked around the control room. No one seemed to be particularly bothered. "So what do we do about this American, Captain?" he asked.

"We leave him be and go somewhere else. If, as I suspect, this is a new boat in transit to the Pacific, he will no doubt continue south and we'll be done with him."

"What if he follows us?"

"Then we shall have to conclude that he is *not* a new boat, and is actually patrolling in this region. If that should be the case, we will have to either get away from him or sink him." He smiled. "I would prefer the first. I would much rather save our torpedoes for more suitable targets."

Henschel walked across the control room to the steering stand. "Make your course zero-nine-eight," he ordered.

*　　　*　　　*

"Enemy is turning, Captain," the sonar operator reported. "Coming around to an easterly heading."

"Give me his course when he steadies up," Billings said. He's trying to get away, he thought. It made sense. A U-boat wouldn't want to fight unless he had to. If *Mako* had blundered across his sights the U-boat's captain would probably have taken the shot, but he wouldn't intentionally get into a fight with an enemy who knew he was there. It really didn't matter what navy you were in, submariners were sneaky bastards who didn't believe in fighting fair. Fighting fair mostly got you killed.

"Enemy course appears to be about zero-niner-seven, Captain. Speed three knots, bearing three-eight-one, range three-one-two-seven."

Billings bent over the chart table. He was here, and the enemy was there and heading that way. "Steer one-four-eight," he ordered. "Make turns for five knots."

"Steer one-four-eight, aye. Course is one-four-eight. Speed five knots."

If he'd calculated correctly, the new course would find *Mako* crossing the U-boats's course about a thousand yards astern. The goal was to stay close enough to shoot once the U-boat surfaced. Despite what a couple of movies had suggested, there was no practical way for one submerged submarine to attack another. You had to be able to see what you were shooting at.

* * *

Now we know, Henschel thought. The American boat was following them around. That likely meant that it was not a new boat on the way to the Pacific, but on a local patrol. Or at least on transit from one east coast port to another. Whichever it was, the fact that her captain was clearly pursuing *U-395* meant that Henschel was going to have to find a way to either get away or work into a position where he could attack. A new boat would probably avoid contact. So, for that matter, would any *sensible* submarine captain. Hunting an alerted enemy carried too much risk. That probably meant he was on patrol.

How long could the American stay submerged? That was the key here. So long as they were submerged, there wasn't much either could do to the other, short of an accidental collision. Both would avoid that. There would be no winner in a collision. So it came down to submerged endurance. The boat that surfaced first would become the target.

Far better, Henschel thought, to separate and each go his own way. That would be his preference, to somehow escape the American's detection gear and slip away. He would sink the American if it came to that, but his mission would be better served by breaking contact. The American boats, at least the newer ones, were big, capable of staying under water for nearly three days before they would be forced to surface for air.

But what about battery capacity? The Americans had been running on their main engines when they were detected. Most likely they had a fully charged battery. How long could they run on batteries, and how fast?

The only thing he was really sure of was that his boat could almost certainly go deeper. But not here. In this area they would find the bottom before either of them came close to their maximum diving depth.

He made a decision. "Come to new course one-eight-zero," he ordered. "Reduce to two knots. Depth five-zero meters. Silent routine."

U-395's best chance would be to disappear. He would head due south for a few minutes at two knots and hope the American sound man lost contact. At two knots the screws would be as close to silent as possible without shutting off the motors. Any slower and they would find it difficult to steer and maintain depth.

"Now," he said, looking at Krause, "we see how alert these Americans are."

* * *

"Enemy is changing course," Williams said, looking up from the sonar stack. "Seems to be reducing speed as well."

"Which way?" The Krauts were pretty smart, Billings thought. It would

24

be just like them to come up with a way of shooting at a submerged sub.

"He's swinging around toward the south."

Still heading away from us, then, Billings thought. Good. "Keep on him, Williams."

"Aye, aye, sir."

"Trying to get away," Norris said.

If I had any sense, Billings thought, I'd be doing the same thing. "Safest course for him, XO," he said. He probably wants to save his torpedoes for another tanker, and he has to recognize that there's always a chance we could get him."

"Enemy seems to have steadied up on one-eight-zero," Williams reported. "Getting very faint."

Billings was busy with the protractor and parallel rules. "New course one-niner-five," he ordered. "Reduce to three knots." That should bring them back onto the U-boat's tail. Reducing speed would make their own boat a little quieter, slightly reduce the noise of the water passing around the hydrophones and increase the range a few yards. He wasn't concerned with catching up; he just wanted to stay close enough to catch the U-boat when it came up for air or to charge batteries.

*   *   *

"How long have we been at this, Hermann?" Henschel asked.

The IWO looked at his watch. "Fifteen hours, Captain."

"And that American bastard is still following us. LI, battery?"

"Perhaps another three hours, Captain, presuming we don't have to increase speed."

"What time is it?"

"1500 local time," Krause said.

"Daylight," Henschel mused. "And it will still be several hours before dark when we run out of power."

"Perhaps we should consider setting down on the bottom and reducing power enough that the batteries will make it to dark?"

"If that American sub wasn't there, I would consider this. But as long as we keep moving he's going to stay submerged chasing us. If we sit on the bottom you can bet he'll quickly surface and get on his wireless. If the situation were reversed, I can tell you that I'd be calling in a few destroyers, telling them where to look, and then getting out of the way. I am sure he would do the same."

"Something needs to happen soon," Krause said. "I have a ghastly headache, and am beginning to feel a little drunk. We are running out of oxygen, or perhaps there is too much carbon dioxide in the boat now."

"It hardly matters which, does it? Before too much longer we will have to surface, even if only to the extent of broaching the bridge hatch and running an engine long enough to replace the air in the boat."

Krause frowned. "I don't suppose we should be so fortunate as to find a nice thunder storm."

"Probably a lovely day," Henschel said. "Unfortunately."

*   *   *

Williams was hunched over the sonar stack, his hand pressing the headphones into his ears. "Sounds like he's flooding a tube," he reported.

Billings looked across the chart table at Norris. Now what? "Do you suppose he has one of those homing fish we've heard about?"

"I'd think he'd have used it by now if he did."

Billings yawned. He didn't feel tired, but CO_2 was building up in the boat. *Mako* carried bottled oxygen, which could be released into the air, but it was the CO_2 buildup that really caused the problems. They'd already spread the absorbent. It helped, but not enough. They were going to need fresh air before long.

"I don't want to let this guy get away, but if he doesn't surface very soon that may be the only sensible course of action."

"Enemy opening outer door," Williams reported. "Enemy has fired. Torpedo in the water."

"Depth?" Billings demanded.

"Five-eight-two," Reilly reported. The question was perhaps a bit equivocal, but the COB had instantly decided that the captain would be perfectly aware of his own depth and wanted to know where the bottom was.

"Bearing on torpedo?"

"Zero-four-two."

"Range to target. Ping him."

"Two-five-three-two."

So he had a little time. Not a lot, but he could take a few seconds and see what was happening. "Bearing on torpedo."

"Zero-four-niner."

Billings could hear the relief in Williams' voice. The bearing was opening. The torpedo was going to miss. In a collision situation you didn't worry about opening or closing bearings, you worried about *steady* bearings. A steady bearing meant a collision, opening or closing meant a miss.

"He can't really have expected to hit us, can he?" Norris mused.

Billings shook his head. "No. But he certainly got our attention, didn't he?"

So what is he up to? Billings wondered. Trying to scare us away? Or trying to distract us?

"Bearing on torpedo?"

"One-two-two."

So ignore the torpedo. "What's the U-boat doing?"

"Maintaining course and speed. No—hull popping!"

"He's coming up," Billings said. "He's trying to keep us busy while he comes up on his planes."

Time to take some chances. "Increase to four knots. Periscope depth."

Mako headed up.

*   *   *

There were times, Henschel thought, when you had no choice but to take the risk. They had no more than twenty minutes on the batteries, and if this was going to work they needed full speed *before* the boat reached the surface and they could start the engines.

He didn't dare blow the ballast tanks before surfacing. That would be too obvious—too noisy. Better to force the boat to the surface using the planes, and only when the bridge hatch was clear to blow the tanks, with the boat already working up to full speed. The engines probably wouldn't like it very much, starting and immediately going to flank speed, but the alternative was probably to be sunk anyway. Engines could be rebuilt, a pressure hull with a torpedo hole in it could not.

"Fourteen meters, Captain."

Henschel was already in the tower, along with the three bridge lookouts. They were at periscope depth and going up like an express elevator, though on almost an even keel.

"Bridge is clear!"

Henschel spun the locking wheel part way, feeling the hatch rise a few centimeters while the conning tower echoed with the scream of compressed air escaping around the gasket. After being submerged for eighteen hours he didn't dare open the hatch without letting the pressure vent. Otherwise he might find himself spit out and injured.

The scream of escaping air stopped and Henschel spun the wheel the rest of the way, shoving the hatch open and rushing up the ladder onto the dripping deck. He didn't take time to look around; the enemy was either ready or not and there wasn't a damned thing he could do about it. The lookouts would have to keep an eye on things for the first minute or so.

He snapped open the voice pipe. "Start main engines. Both ahead flank! Blow main ballast."

He looked down at the repeaters. *U-395* was doing eight knots on the remains of the charge. Once the diesels were on line he could add another ten or eleven knots to that. *U-395* had managed 20 knots on her trials, but that was right from the builder, with an absolutely clean bottom.

Both engines caught at once. Back in the engine room Rosenberg would be matching the engine speed to the motors, throwing in the clutches, and then feeding the fuel oil to the big diesels.

While the engineer brought up the engine speed, the boat was rising in the water as the ballast was expelled. Henschel didn't feel safe on the surface in broad daylight, but at least now he didn't have to worry about trying to hold the boat broached on the planes. With the ballast tanks empty she could float without help.

He looked down at the log repeater. Fourteen knots and rising, course steady on zero-nine-zero. This wasn't the time to be zigging, Henschel thought. Just head out to sea and as fast as possible. Make the American work to catch him. The boat couldn't outrun a torpedo, obviously, yet there was still a chance. If the American took a shot it would take time to set it up, more time to flood the tubes, open the outer doors, and fire.

He didn't have to outrun a torpedo, he just had to be far enough away that it couldn't catch up before it ran out of fuel or the batteries went flat. And if he was really lucky, the Americans would still be trying to get out of the way of the eel he had fired in their direction before sprinting for the surface. Hitting them would be nothing more than a fortunate accident, but he could hope they were at least distracted long enough for him to get away.

*   *   *

"Up 'scope!"

Billings swung the periscope to bear dead ahead. That was where sonar put the German.

And there he was. "On the surface," Billings said, "trimmed well up." He centered the crosshairs on the retreating U-boat. "Bearing—mark!"

"Zero-zero-two."

"Sonar—range?"

"Three-eight-niner-seven."

Damn. Nearly 4,000 yards. He had to get the fish off quick or there would be no chance of catching him.

"Angle on the bow, one-eight-zero," Billings said.

Norris fed the figures into the torpedo data computer.

"This is going to have to be a snap shot," Billings said. "Flood one and two and open outer doors. Spin 'em up and fire as soon as we have a solution light and the fish are ready."

The TDC was sending the gyro data directly to the torpedoes. It took a few seconds for the gyro settings to match.

"Solution light," Norris said.

"Torpedoes set," Reilly reported, his hand poised over the firing button.

"Fire one!"

Reilly pushed the big, mushroom shaped red button. The boat shivered slightly as the Mark 14 torpedo was ejected from the tube.

"Number one fired electrically," Reilly reported.

Billings made himself slowly count to ten. "Fire two!"

"Two fired electrically."

"Sonar?"

"Both fish running hot, straight, and normal."

Billings nodded. Nothing was certain yet. The German might be able to outdistance the fish. All he needed to do was to make another three or four thousand yards before the torpedoes got to him.

"How fast is the target moving?" he asked.

"Estimate eighteen knots."

Billings looked over at Norris. "Let's get this boat on the surface," he said. "We can't chase him down here and I want to get something in the can."

* * *

"Torpedo tracks, dead astern," the after lookout reported.

Henschel swung around and lifted his binoculars. The tracks were clear enough in the nearly calm sea. Perhaps a thousand meters astern and closing at a tremendous rate. Intelligence said that the American wet heater torpedoes ran at about 45 knots.

There were two tracks, roughly parallel. He looked at the gyro repeater. They were still running due east. He looked aft again, his brain automatically calculating angles.

"Come left to zero-eight-five," he ordered. Only a slight course change, but it should be enough.

U-395 turned five degrees north. The first torpedo had seemed to be aimed right at the stern, the second perhaps twenty meters farther to the south. Too big a change might swing the stern into their path; a slight change should veer them slightly to the north of the torpedo tracks. Even a couple meters was probably enough.

"Submarine surfacing," the same lookout reported. "Red one-eight-five. Range about four thousand."

Behind him, Henschel could see the slender attack periscope swinging onto the reported bearing. Beyond it the enemy submarine was surging to the surface.

Henschel bent over the voice pipe. "After room—bridge! Is the stern tube reloaded yet?"

"After room, aye. Another three to four minutes, Captain."

Damn.

Henschel lifted his binoculars and focused on the enemy sub. Not what he had expected. The boat was clearly modern, but it was also obviously much smaller than most American boats. And the bridge was decidedly odd, with a long, enclosed forebridge ringed with circular deadlights. Perhaps they could steer from the bridge, he thought.

His mind wandered just long enough to decide that having a wheel on the bridge would be quite useful in harbor, or when docking, before he dragged his thoughts resolutely back onto the present situation.

Has the American called for help? he wondered. Now that both boats were on the surface, it would be easy enough for the American to light up his wireless and get off a signal.

There were half a dozen men on the American's upper bridge now. At this distance, even with binoculars, he couldn't tell who was the captain. Two of the men wore khaki uniforms, but the Americans didn't have the German tradition of the captain wearing a white cap cover, and it was too far away to see the tiny metal rank insignia they wore on their collars.

Suddenly more men were emerging onto the bridge and dropping down to the main deck, running aft. "In a minute," Henschel told König, "we are going to have a problem. We are just that much too far ahead for him to fire another torpedo, but I suspect we are well within range of his deck gun. He wouldn't put that many men on deck unless he was manning the gun."

"What do we do, Captain?"

"We get the stern tube loaded and put an eel into him before he can get a hit."

"Shouldn't we man our own gun?"

"The gun is on the bow. To fire we would have to turn back, so that we would be *closing* the range. We would also present a bigger target, for it would put us broadside to as we turned. He'll have to do the same to fire at us with an aft mounted gun, but he'll do it first."

"Enemy is turning, Captain," a lookout shouted.

*   *   *

"Target acquired!" the gun captain reported.

Billings nodded, holding the U-boat in his binoculars. "Open fire."

The little 3"/50-calibre gun fired, the shell screaming past the bridge. They had opened fire as soon as the enemy was visible from the gun, which was now trained well ahead of the beam.

Fuller was on the cigarette deck, his binoculars to his eyes. As the most junior officer aboard the job of gunnery officer naturally fell into his lap. At the moment, he was feeling a little uneasy about that. Gunnery officer in a submarine was usually a *very* easy job, because normally there was nothing to shoot at.

A small waterspout lifted up behind the enemy. "Short," Fuller called down. "Up 200. Right 20."

Not too bad for what was really just a snap shot.

Behind the pointer, the sight setter made the adjustments. Another shell went into the breech. They were using HC, high capacity, shells. What the British would have called semi-armour piercing, and the U.S. Navy generally called "common." The 34 pound fixed rounds fired a 13 pound projectile filled with just over a pound and quarter of high explosive. Not much, but more than enough to do some damage to an unarmored target.

Most of the weight was in the tapered nose of the projectile, which had to be strong enough to penetrate a ship's hull before exploding.

"Ready!"

"Fire!"

"Short, up 20."

"Ready!"

"Fire!"

This time there was no splash. The little shell punched a neat hole in the enemy's stern, which immediately became a jagged crater as the charge detonated inside the pressure hull.

"On," Fuller shouted. "Fire for effect!"

*   *   *

"Damage report," Henschel demanded.

"Stern tube out of commission. The shell exploded inside the tube. Minimal damage to the stern room, but the tube is useless."

For the first time in his career, Henschel found himself happy that a torpedo crew hadn't worked as quickly as he would normally wish. If the eel had been in the tube the shell would almost certainly have set off the warhead and it would be all over. As it was… Well, they still had power.

"Right full rudder."

The boat veered to starboard as another shell just missed to port. The enemy was firing as quickly as he could reload.

Henschel bent over the voice pipes. "Forward room, ready all tubes."

There was only one chance now. He would turn quickly, fire all four tubes at the American, and try to get away while the enemy was dodging his torpedoes.

Another hit, further forward. The boat veered suddenly to port as the port engine seized up.

"Engine room — bridge! Report!"

The starboard engine clattered to a stop as a stoker appeared in the bridge hatch. "Direct hit on the engine room, Captain," he reported. "LI is dead. So is most of the duty section. Port engine destroyed. Fuel lines cut to starboard engine."

So much for tactics, Henschel thought. He could still maneuver on batteries, but they hadn't managed to get enough of a charge in the can to make it more than a few miles.

Another shell smashed into the stern. It was time. He turned to the signalman.

"Send to enemy, 'We surrender'."

"How?"

Of course. The man didn't speak English. He spelled it out for him.

One more shell crashed into the ruined engine room as the signalman was sending, and then there were no more.

"Everyone on deck," Henschel ordered. "Crew aft," he added. There was no sense giving the American any room for misinterpretation by allowing anyone forward. Someone might think he was manning the gun and start shooting again.

Krause was the last man up, pushing up the weighted bag with the code books, and the cased Enigma machine, ahead of him. These went over the side.

Henschel looked aft, counting heads. Twelve men were still below. They would remain there forever.

The enemy was approaching cautiously, crabwise, to keep the deck gun in battery. Henschel could see four heavy machine-guns and a 20 mm Oerlikon trained on his boat.

*   *   *

Billings hove to a little over 20 yards from the enemy. "Rig scrambling nets," he ordered. "They're going to have to swim across."

While this was being done, he switched on the loud hailer. "Do you speak English?" he called.

"Yes." It was the officer in the white cap. That would make him the captain, Billing remembered. Just as well he had survived, it would make this easier. Intelligence had reported that U-boat captains were required to speak English. He wondered how well.

"Have your men swim across. We will not come any closer."

"Understood."

There was a flurry of German and the crew began to jump into the water. They were all wearing life vests, so Billings wasn't worried about non-swimmers. If there were any, their pals could tow them.

The men on the bridge were the last to go into the water. Billings noticed the captain look at his watch, and caught a nod from the other officer.

"Bridge—radio. *Culpepper* reports he's 35 minutes from our position."

"Bridge, aye. Thank you."

So, Billings thought, he wouldn't have to entertain the Germans for long. The old destroyer would be there soon, and she would have better facilities for handling the prisoners.

The COB escorted the white capped officer onto the bridge. The prisoner saluted and Billings returned it. You still had to maintain the formalities.

"I am *Kapitänleutnant* Otto Henschel. I wish to thank you for picking up my crew. And for ceasing fire when we signaled." The gratitude for the latter was genuine; Henschel was fairly sure that a British ship would have kept shooting.

"Did you get everyone off?"

"All but twelve men. They were killed by your shells."

Billings nodded. "There's a destroyer on the way to collect you and your men and take you into port. I imagine they'll put a boarding party aboard your boat."

Henschel looked at his watch. "I do not think so, Captain. Myself, and my men, we surrender. I see no reason to commit suicide. My boat, however..."

They heard the first explosion two minutes later. There were a total of four. These were small explosions, but the charges had been carefully placed at hull fittings. It didn't take much to shatter piping and valves. The Atlantic flowed unimpeded into the hull.

U-395 went under ten minutes before the *Culpepper* arrived.

When the destroyer came alongside and began to take off the Germans, a seaman was already painting a small German naval ensign on the little submarine's bridge. Billings looked down at it and smiled.

Even if it was mostly luck, he had accomplished something. He would probably get that Pacific boat now, and his men would be able to wear the combat patrol pin and swagger a little when they arrived at their next boats.

All in all, he thought, not bad for what they had all presumed would be just another pointless patrol.

ELEMENT OF SURPRISE

[This story was written back in the mid-1970s, when I was busy creating the Gehunite civilisation. Two novels resulted, *Alura*, which was very long, and *The Highest Honour*, which was a bit shorter. Neither of those survives, though I do still have carbons of the first part of the latter. *Alura* was swords and sorcery, with an unusual intrusion of actual science here and there. *The Highest Honour* was set a few hundred years later, when the Gehunite culture had begun to resemble our own, complete with aeroplanes, nuclear warships, and a nasty war between a world spanning Gehunite Empire and small, isolated, and thoroughly nasty Arzucalda. This wasn't *Star Wars*; the Imperial forces were the good guys. Being set in a completely different civilisation, there are obvious differences in things such as time keeping and dates, including a 30 hour day with 100 minutes to the hour, a 300 degree circle, and a thirteen month year with 28 days in each month and two extra-weekly holidays every year to make up the difference.]

I t was night, and the giant warship ploughed serenely through the long Western Ocean rollers, her four escorting destroyers keeping perfect station in the bright moonlight.

High up in the great vessel's pilothouse, Captain Eno Karnamo sat back in his tall, wooden chair, his grey eyes shut, as if he were sleeping. In his mind he was at home, in the old fieldstone house close by the great Koril Harbour Naval Base, on Tufaria Bay, a few miles from Salmik. The pilothouse clock, set to local time, read 29:93, which meant that it would be nine hours later, just nearing dawn, back in Salmik.

"Seven more minutes," he heard Lieutenant Ehnurti say, "and we can put 381 behind us."

The captain smiled. At home it would already be nearly nine hours into the New Year's Holiday, and his wife, Sami, who kept a strict schedule on *all* days, would be rousting the children from their beds. Well, he thought, if you don't want an enforced routine, you shouldn't marry a colour sergeant of Imperial Marines. Not that he had any complaints; she was a damn good wife, even if she was still the old drill instructor in some areas.

And it wouldn't hurt the children a bit to get up early, holiday or no.

Stifling a yawn, Karnamo stood up and walked forward to peer through the thick, bullet-resistant screen. In the moonlight, the bow stood out quite clearly as it cut through the long rollers, while closer he could see the two forward turrets, with their triple-mount 457 MM guns. The most powerful armament ever carried by an Imperial battleship. Even the secondary battery, consisting of eight 280 MM guns, was more powerful than a heavy cruiser.

Yet his ship was hopelessly obsolete. His Imperial Majesty's Battleship *Dushlin* was the first, and last, of her class, completed just in time for the Navy to realise that carrier aircraft had rendered the whole concept of the line of battle a relic.

Like himself. Obsolete, left behind by progress. A few years earlier this would have been the most sought-after command in the Imperial Navy. The most powerful battleship in the world, capable of circling the world dozens of times without stopping on her four nuclear reactors, her thick armour more than adequate protection against lesser ships.

And now? Now the carriers were the plum commands, and even HIMS *Dushlin* little more than a floating museum piece. Useful enough for shore bombardment, should another war happen to break out, but for now relegated to training duties.

He smiled tightly. At least he had a command. In peacetime that fact was worth something. His wife had retired two years ago, not because of their family—the Service made more than adequate provision for issues of that type—but because it had become clear she was unlikely to be promoted to sergeant major before mandatory retirement.

Well, Karnamo thought, I'll retire as a captain, won't I? He had five years left on his 30. Flag rank was unlikely, to say the least.

The clock showed 30:00 exactly. Midnight. The start of a new year, the 382nd since the founding of the Gehunite Empire by Salmik the Great.

"Happy New Year, sir!" Lieutenant Ehnurti said.

"Happy New Year, Gora," Karnamo replied.

Signal lanterns were blinking on the escorting destroyers, passing the usual new year wishes for good health, long life, and the return of the rum ration. At the plot table, Lieutenant Ehnurti, as officer of the watch, was now pondering the deck log, wondering if she could think of something witty to mark the arrival of the new year. It wasn't the wit that was eluding her; tradition said the entry should be in verse. She was an excellent navigator, but not much of a poet.

The intercom squealed. "Bridge...radar!"

Reprieve, Ehnurti thought. "Bridge, aye."

"Bridge, I have radar contact bearing amber oh-five, range five-four-four."

Ehnurti leaned over the grill. "Contact amber oh-five, range five-four-four, aye." She looked over at the captain.

Karnamo shrugged. Probably nothing important, he thought. In peacetime all you really had to worry about was running into something. That wasn't much of a worry in *Dushlin*, with the search radar mounted nearly three metres higher than in any other ship in the world. The designers had ensured that she would always be the first to know if she had company.

The watch continued quietly now, the frantic exchange of signals completed until next year.

A signals rating came through the door, looking like he'd just seen a ghost. He was trembling as he handed the captain a decoded signal. What the hell was the matter with the man? Karnamo wondered.

Then he read the signal.

SUIMEHREON HARBOUR UNDER HEAVY ATTACK BY ARZUCALDAN CARRIER AIRCRAFT FROM 00:10 HOURS. HEAVY DAMAGE. ALL UNITS ASSUME FULL WAR FOOTING AS FROM RECEIPT OF THIS SIGNAL. FOIC, SUIMEHREON HARBOUR.

For a moment he felt unable to move. Then, with a convulsive shake of his head, he dashed across the pilothouse and stabbed the red button under the screen, setting the alarm bells ringing throughout the ship and the crew pouring out of their berths and racing for their action stations.

Karnamo picked up a handset. "What do you make of that radar contact?" he asked, when the operator came on the line.

"Ten ships, sir," the operator replied. "Four of them fairly large, and moving all in formation. Someone else out on exercise, I'd guess."

"Could they be carriers, do you think?"

"Possibly, sir. They're arranged as you'd expect with four carriers and six escorts. But I don't see any aircraft in the area."

"Thank you." Karnamo replaced the handset. "Captain has the conn. Come right five degrees," he ordered. "Increase to flank. Signal escorts to conform."

"Aye, aye. New course is one-five-five, sir."

"The destroyers won't be able to keep up, sir," Ehnurti said. *Dushlin* was huge, and even at that overpowered. She would be doing nearly 49 knots at flank speed. Unless a vessel could plane, waterline length determined maximum speed, which meant that the much smaller destroyers would be limited to around 39 knots.

"They'll do their best," Karnamo said. "And once we get to work they can catch us up."

Commander Raschnur, the second-in-command, burst through the door, still zipping up his working uniform. He had been sound asleep when the alarm bells started clanging. "What's going on, sir?" he asked.

"War, Commander. We've had a signal the base is being attacked at this moment."

"What about us, sir?"

"Radar has located what appears to be the enemy's carrier task force. L'Mik willing, we may just be able to do some damage before they sink us."

"Arzucalda?"

Karnamo shrugged. "So the signal says. Who else could it be? Callaa has only coastal forces, and they've been allies for hundreds of years. Feria will remain neutral until doomsday, and Kaam—well, their biggest ship is an anti-submarine carrier that can't fly off fixed-wing aeroplanes. It has to be Arzucalda."

"I've never trusted Kinmon," Raschnur said.

"No. Their king had no idea what he was doing when he made that man chancellor."

"He found out soon enough."

He had indeed, Karnamo thought. Within a year of being installed in the Arzucaldan chancellor's office, Alver Kinmon had got legislation passed that reduced the monarchy to mere figurehead status. Ostensibly, King Korzal IX was the Arzucaldan head of state. Actually, he was just a government employee in a nice uniform.

"Forty-eight knots, sir."

Not quite what she'd done on trials, but respectable enough, Karnamo thought.

Now the dark waters were flung high as the great battleship tore through the waves, her escorting destroyers slowly dropping back, unable to keep up even with their reactors at full power.

"In range in two minutes."

"Reduce to half speed," Karnamo ordered. He wondered if the Arzucaldans had included submarines in their attack force.

Then the enemy task force was visible from the main rangefinder station, high atop the superstructure. Four carriers, definitely Arzucaldan, with six powerful fleet destroyers riding herd. With the bright moonlight, and the image enhancer built into the rangefinder, it was almost like daylight to the gunnery officer.

He turned his dial and a faint green light appeared over the letter "we," for "weehmiti," main. The light was still red over the secondary armament indicator.

"In range with main battery," the gunnery officer reported.

"Stand by to engage," Karnamo ordered.

"Standing by, sir. Main battery on central control."

The armoured shutters slid down over the thick windows. Karnamo would have preferred to direct the action from the open bridge, on the next higher level, but the tremendous muzzle blast of the main guns made that out of the question. The shutters were as much to protect the screen from that muzzle blast as to keep out enemy shells.

"Open fire," he ordered.

It was like the end of the world. The huge ship seemed to leap sideways as the nine great guns fired as one, slamming back on their springs, and the moonlit night vanished in the glare of the muzzle flashes.

*   *   *

Admiral Torgun Yorgal stood silently on the flag bridge of the Arzucaldan Republican Fleet Carrier *Restless*, a pleased smile on his face as the reports came in from the attacking squadrons. He had taken a calculated risk in sending off every plane in the task force on the attack, and it seemed to be paying off. Later in the war, he would never dare risk it, but now there were no enemy carriers at sea to oppose him. According to intelligence, the only enemy units at sea in this area were training ships, crewed mostly by fourth year naval cadets. He felt safe enough.

"It's going better than we dared hope," the chief-of-staff was saying. "We caught them completely by surprise. Their fighters never even made it into the air."

"Yes, it's the same at Koril Harbour and Gorbindar. Complete surprise."

"This war will be over before it's started, sir." The chief-of-staff was looking at reports. "Five carriers in harbour, attacked and out of action. Seven battleships in harbour, all out of action. Three heavy cruisers..."

"How many battleships?"

"Seven."

"There should be eight."

Far off to port, the black horizon erupted like a volcano.

"What the hell was that?" the chief-of-staff sputtered.

The admiral shook his head. "There should have been eight."

"What?"

"Only a training ship, they said."

"What?"

They ducked involuntarily as the nine great shells roared overhead with the sound of a passing train.

"Great gods!"

The admiral turned just as the leading carrier, *Victorious*, reeled under the impact of the broadside. Three shells straddled the huge ship, but the other six slammed into her flight deck and tore through several more before exploding deep in her hull. One of the 1,100 kilogram shells exploded in *Victorious'* main magazine.

The ship simply vanished in the explosion that followed.

The admiral thought of the planes which would even now be flying back to the task force. Useless to him, he thought, all of their bombs and torpedoes expended in the attack. They would have to land and rearm instantly to deal with this new threat.

He cringed as a second broadside splashed harmlessly into the empty ocean, where *Victorious* would have been if she hadn't blown up. So the

Gehunite gunnery officer was confident enough of his aim to have two salvos in the air at the same time.

Perhaps more to the point, the gunnery crews were good enough to accomplish that feat. This wasn't a training ship. Or, if it was, there were regular navy men handling the guns. Fourth year cadets, Intelligence had said. Officers in training, by now only a few months from graduation. But they would be training to perform officers' duties; the greatest part of the crew, the seamen and Marines, the men and women whose job was to maintain and fight the ship, they would be regulars.

He wondered if his planes would have anywhere to land when they got back.

Perfect surprise, he thought. If his planes had surprised Suimehreon Harbour, then it seemed the Imperial Navy still had a surprise waiting for him as well. Why hadn't Intelligence said that the training cruise was in a bloody battleship?

      *   *   *

"Shift to target two," the gunnery officer snapped. "Number one has blown up."

How can he sound so bloody calm? Karnamo wondered. It's all I can do to keep from leaping into the air. Tell me this ship is obsolete now!

Deep in the bowels of the ship a senior gunnery rating bent over the big radar repeater and carefully moved the aiming point onto the second target. The flip of a switch locked it on, and now the computers would take over, keeping the great guns locked on the target, compensating for the slightest movement of either ship.

"Target two locked on," she reported.

"Fire!"

Nine more 1,100 kilogram shells started on their way.

"Six smaller targets separating from main force," a rating reported. "Coming this way."

In the director, the gunnery officer had seen this. The enemy admiral was sending his destroyers to intercept. They could present a problem if they got close enough to fire torpedoes. Their guns would hardly amount to a nuisance, but a torpedo in the wrong place could be trouble.

"Secondary battery, engage destroyers."

      *   *   *

Radar picked up the first returning planes an hour later. By that time, only one of the Arzucaldan carriers remained afloat. Karnamo was developing a grudging admiration for that captain, who seemed to be a bit sharper than all the others. He had learnt to wait until he saw the muzzle flashes, then make a drastic course change. They were still firing at extreme range—Karnamo saw no good reason to close the range and risk a torpedo from the two Arzucaldan destroyers which had so far managed to stay out of the way of *Dushlin*'s secondary battery, but were still being kept far enough away to make a torpedo attack pointless—so it took the great shells nearly two minutes to reach their target. Time enough to elude, so long as you could guess where the shells wouldn't be.

Meanwhile, *Dushlin*'s gunnery officer was busily trying to guess which way the Arzucaldan captain would turn next.

At last, one hour and seventy minutes after the battle was joined, one of the big shells smashed through the carrier's stern. It didn't explode until it had passed through the hull, but the effect was more than enough. In ripping through the stern, the shell had smashed one of the hydraulic rams that controlled the rudder, and the detonation of the delayed fuse 30 metres under the hull opened seams and broke a blade off the port outer screw, forcing the engineers to shut down that shaft.

With the rudder jammed, the carrier could only steam in a huge circle. Her captain, recognising the inevitable result, struck his flag, rang down all stop, and signalled his surrender.

The two destroyers, presumably still capable of fighting, reversed course and headed for the fleet rendezvous point a thousand miles to the west. After quickly signalling Suimehreon Harbour with his results, Karnamo closed on the surrendered carrier. The admiral agreed that it was best to let the destroyers get away.

He didn't expect them to get far. If they stayed anywhere near the course Karnamo had reported them taking, they would run into *Marauder* shortly after daybreak. The *Warrior* class attack sub would make short work of them.

"Have our escorts start looking for survivors," Karnamo ordered. "And tell our own lookouts to keep their eyes open, too."

"What about the planes, sir?" Ehnurti asked.

"I shouldn't think they can do much now."

Nor could they. With their bombs and torpedoes expended, and nothing to fight with except the machine-guns in the leading edges of their wings, the planes posed no threat at all to the armoured giant that was now idling near the damaged *Intrepid*. As they ran out of fuel, the planes began to ditch, far enough from the two big ships not to appear threatening, but close enough that there was a good chance of being picked up.

*   *   *

The Commander found Karnamo is his sea cabin after the last airman had been picked up. The ship was moving again, zig zagging as it made a wide circuit around the damaged enemy carrier.

"All the enemy pilots have been ferried over to the carrier," Raschnur said. "They've got more room. I've also sent over most of our Marine detachment, just to keep them from getting rowdy. The plumber says it'll be a dockyard job to fix the carrier's steering gear, so I don't think we need to worry about them trying to get away."

"I've spoken to Flag," Karnamo said. "They're sending a big fleet tug out to collect the carrier. I suppose they'll fix her up and add her to our own fleet."

"That'll be a job, sir. They'll need to replace the reactors. The Arzu-caldans apparently have a lot to learn about safety. So says Commander Niorazen, at least."

Niorazen was *Dushlin*'s chief engineer. "He would know."

"What about us?"

"Back to base as soon as our relief arrives."

"You know, sir," the Commander said, "I never really thought we could do it. It's not supposed to be possible. A battleship with no air cover against a carrier task force."

"I don't think it will ever happen again. I've talked to *Intrepid*'s captain. His admiral was convinced there was no one out here who could harm him, so he sent every plane he had on the attack. The truth is, what we did was impossible. Once we're back in harbour I doubt this ship will venture out again without a carrier along for protection." He smiled. "But you'll have to admit, it was fun."

SURVIVOR

The first torpedo struck the ship at the bulkhead between number one and two fire rooms. There was no hope from that point, with the sea pouring into both compartments. The second torpedo, striking the ship forward, simply insured that the end would come more quickly.

Of the 293 officers and men aboard, only 87 went into the water. The rest went down with the ship, which took less than two minutes to go from a swift, vital fleet unit to just another wreck on the bottom of the Pacific.

Jim Jenkins, one of the lucky ones, floated in his life vest, watching dispassionately as his ship disappeared beneath the roiling water. It was 1900 hours, he noted, so it would be dark soon. Around him, the other survivors seemed equally lethargic, as if everything had happened too quickly for most of them to even realize the mess they were in.

Or that they had survived.

About twenty men were crowded into one of the canvas-covered balsa rafts. It was an indication of how quickly destruction had come that there was only one—the rest had gone down with the ship, still securely lashed to their launching rails.

After a time, Jenkins began to look around for any sign of the submarine that had killed his ship. He wasn't sure if he wanted to find it, for it would undoubtedly be Japanese, and its commander would be as likely to order that survivors be shot in the water as he was to save anyone.

Why the hell couldn't we be in the Atlantic? Jenkins wondered. At least the Krauts don't shoot survivors.

"Jim! You okay?"

Jenkins turned his head, paddling around to see who was talking. It turned out to be Curtis, who berthed in the same compartment. "I think so," he replied. "You?"

"All things considered, yeah."

"What the hell happened, Bob?"

"Last I knew, I was walking along the starboard side, and then I'm flying through the air and taking a swim. I found the life jacket floating in the water."

"I had time to get mine," Jenkins said, "but that's about it. Everything else went down with the ship."

"Sub?"

"Had to be. A single explosion could have been a mine, but we were hit twice. That says torpedo. I just hope the sub went away."

Curtis looked around. "Yeah. Damned Nips wouldn't be too likely to pick us up, would they?"

Jenkins shook his head. "Not likely at all." He looked at the western horizon. "It'll be dark soon. We'd better get organized or people are likely to drift away during the night."

"Are there any officers here?"

"Haven't seen any." Jenkins looked to his right, into the gathering darkness. There was little twilight in these waters, and when darkness came it came swiftly. "Let's swim over by the raft. If we stay together there'll be a lot better chance we'll all get picked up when they come looking for us."

Curtis frowned. "Assuming they do. The ship went down awful fast. Do you think there was time to get a message off?"

"Even if there wasn't, I'm going to presume that there was. I don't think I want to be floating around out here without at least a little hope." He started swimming. "Come on."

The two men swam awkwardly, hampered by their bulky life vests. It took several minutes to make the eighty yards to the raft, and when they arrived they found that most of the others had had the same idea.

The only officer to be found was Lieutenant Hansen, the supply officer. Separated from his requisition forms, mess bills, and supply tables, he wasn't likely to be of much use.

But they also found Chief Boatswain's Mate Tom Carson in the raft. He was probably worth a dozen officers in this sort of situation, Jenkins thought. Certainly he could contribute more than the pork chop, who sometimes seemed to have trouble remembering which side of the ship was port.

"You men in the water, hang on to the hand ropes," Carson said. "If you can't do that, tie yourself to someone who can. We need to stay together during the night."

Jenkins and Curtis hooked their arms though the big loops of rope that ran around the outside of the raft. It was going to be a long night, Jenkins thought.

His mind wandered back to his hometown, far from the sea, in the middle of the Kansas prairie. At the time the war started his only worry had been whether his girl, Suzy, would like the necklace he'd bought her for Christmas. They'd been going together since high school, and were planning to marry in June, 1942.

The war had changed that. Instead of waiting, they'd got the license and been married within two weeks.

And now he was here, and Suzy was back in Kansas, no doubt worried sick even without knowing his ship had just been sunk. She hadn't wanted him to join up, but had eventually conceded that it was probably better that he did. His number of up, and he would have been drafted before long, and they both figured the Navy was a better option than slogging through the mud with the infantry.

Now he wasn't so sure. At least in the infantry you didn't have to worry about being sunk.

Darkness had come, and the sky was filled with millions of stars. It was something that always seemed to astonish the city boys, when they first went to sea. Growing up in the country, far from any city lights, Jenkins had noticed little change.

The moon would be up in another hour, but for now it was pitch black, the only illumination coming from the stars, and the rescue lights attached to their life vests. Only a few of the men had them turned on now.

In the dark, floating in the warm water, Jenkins found himself nodding off. He hooked his arm more securely in the hand rope. If he fell asleep the vest would keep his head out of the water, but he didn't want to lose his grip and float away. His mind still refused to accept the possibility that someone hadn't managed to get off a distress message.

Someone will be looking for us, he thought. Even if there was no message, the ship was due in at Tinian around dawn, so when she didn't arrive they'd know something had happened and send out search planes.

As Jenkins' chin dropped onto his chest, he was startled back to wakefulness by a sudden cry from the other side of the raft. A yell of pain and fear, but cut off an instant later, as if a door had been shut.

"What the hell was that?" he wondered, speaking aloud in his semiwakeful condition.

Curtis shook his head. "Hell if I know. Bad dream, I hope."

"Yeah."

But there were other reasons a man might cry out in the night, floating in the South Pacific. Most of them unpleasant—some of them had very sharp teeth.

It was said that the sharks had learned to come to the sound of explosions at sea, knowing that there would be men in the water. It wasn't malicious intent on the part of the sharks—men didn't belong in the water, and the sharks didn't know the difference between a thinking, intelligent man and a dumb fish. Both were nothing more than food so far as the shark was concerned.

Five minutes later, there was another cry. So that was it, Jenkins thought. They were no longer alone.

All the stories were going through his mind now. Advice on what to do in this kind of mess. Kick your feet, one idea ran, because if you kick the shark in the snout he'll go away.

But others said just the opposite. Stay as motionless as you possibly could, they said. Sharks hunt out anything that's moving, and thrashing about makes them think they've found an injured fish. Easy prey.

If you need to go, don't. They'll be attracted by the smell.

The moon was coming up now, casting a pale glow on the gently rolling sea. A few feet away, a man was floating in his life vest, his eyes bulged out, mouth open, head lolling. He was rocking oddly in the swell, and Jenkins realized that most of his body was probably gone below the surface.

"What the hell do we do now?" he asked, not really expecting an answer. They were all in the same situation, with only the men in the raft relatively safe. Earlier, there had been talk of rotating men in and out of the raft, giving those in the water a chance to rest, but the arrival of the sharks had probably finished that idea. The men in the water would be willing to get out of it, but he couldn't imagine that anyone *in* the raft would agree to go for a swim.

Something brushed against his leg, shoving him roughly to the left, and an instant later the man floating ten feet in front of him rose a foot out of the water, then was suddenly pulled under, without even the time to cry out.

After what seemed an eternity, but was probably no more than a second or two, the man shot up out of the water, turning in the air before falling back. His body ended just below his ribs, and Jenkins turned away, afraid to look. He could face enemy guns and torpedoes, but this was something else. He was surrounded by killers—killers who would think of him, if they thought of him at all, as nothing more than food.

With each passing minute he became more unsure. Curtis hadn't said anything for hours, his expression in the moonlight declaring that here was a man who could no longer cope, and would re-emerge into the world only when the danger was past. He was looking off into the far distance, and the distance was where safety would be found. The distance *was* safety.

Jenkins just wanted a deck under his feet. Something between him and the pointed dorsal fins that were moving through the floating sailors.

Then it was light. Jenkins realized that he must have fallen asleep during the night, yet couldn't imagine how that might have happened. Was it possible to be so tired that you could sleep while your friends were being eaten around you? Could exhaustion really overcome the instinct for self-preservation?

Evidently it could, he thought.

Around him, shredded life vests floated on the placid sea. Here and there were bodies—parts of bodies—still floating in their vests, perhaps even looking like survivors until you realized that they were floating too high, nothing more than a torso, with the rest of the man digesting in the belly of a shark.

He wondered how many were still alive. Chief Carson had taken a count before dark, finding 87 men, including the twenty-two men crowded into the raft.

Jenkins could count no more than fifteen others in the water he could be sure were alive.

Now he was thirsty, too, surrounded by water, and yet with nothing to drink, like the shipwrecked mariner of Coleridge's poem. The sky was still clear, so there would be no rain, and the survivors would now have to endure the full force of the tropical sun.

Aboard the raft, Lieutenant Hansen was already showing the effects. As the only officer, he was nominally in charge, even if Chief Carson was really running things. His eyes told the story for, like Curtis, he seemed to be looking far over the horizon, staring at some fixed point in space.

But Curtis was starting to come out of it now, sunrise bringing some psychological relief. It was as if, now that he could see again, his mind was assuring him that everything would be okay.

"You okay?" Jenkins asked.

Curtis looked at him, his torso jerking as he moved his limbs. He smiled weakly. "Everything still seems to be there," he said. "So I guess so."

Jenkins looked around. "I don't think we can take another night like that," he said.

Curtis nodded. "Too many gone already, Jim," he agreed. "Makes for bad odds. The fewer of us there are, the more likely we are to be next."

"Yeah."

The day dragged on, the sun blazing down on their exposed faces. Not having any other option, Jenkins eventually urinated into his shorts, the relief from emptying his over-filled bladder nervously counterbalanced by the possibility that the "experts" were right, and it really *would* attract sharks.

His face felt as if the skin was ready to fall off, burned by the sun, and irritated by the salt water. His tongue was swelling, too, as he felt the effects of dehydration while floating in billions of gallons of undrinkable seawater.

It was just after 1400 when he saw an odd reflection in the sea, perhaps a thousand yards from where he was floating, still linked to the raft, with his arm though one of the hand ropes. At first he thought it was just the sun, reflecting off an errant wave, but as it drew nearer he realized that it was the reflection from the upper lens of a submarine's periscope.

Was this how it was going to end? Had the Jap skipper decided to come back and finish everyone off?

The periscope drew closer. Then, after what seemed like hours, a second mast rose behind it, with a cross bar and two stubby wire antennae on it. The crossbar rotated slowly on the mast, and then the periscope began to rise from the sea, followed in moments by the upper structure of a submarine's conning tower fairwater.

"Oh, Christ," Curtis mutter weakly. "He's one of ours."

Jenkins didn't speak. He just nodded, his body shaking as he realized he had survived.

THE COLLINSVILLE UFO

[This piece was written for a collection of "strange and unusual true events," none of which were really true. While there is a long tradition of this sort of thing—every collection of "true supernatural events" ever published is mostly composed of tall tales, outright lies, and wildly exaggerated natural phenomena—I decided to use this story here mostly due to the realization that far too many people would probably believe this nonsense, even when it contains interviews with dead people obtained by having the current incarnation of their spirit undergo hypnotic regression. Given the gullibility of so many people—you'd be surprised how many think that *Ghost Whisperer* is plausible, and that the so-called medium who came up with the idea for the show *really* talks to ghosts—I had my doubts that even marketing the book as fiction would be enough to forestall this.]

On June 3, 1847, the little town of Collinsville, Indiana was thrown into an uproar by the appearance of a flying object in the sky. According to the *Collinsville Advertiser:*

At 3 o'clock yesterday afternoon, as your correspondent was completing the printing of the daily edition, my attention was captured by the pounding of many feet on the recently laid slate sidewalk at the front of the *Advertiser* Building. Going out to inquire as to the reason for this commotion, I was informed by Mr. Alexander Carrington, of the Carrington Dry Goods Emporium, that a report of a flying object had been brought into his store by a neighborhood lad, and that he, together with several individuals who had been in his shop, were rushing out to see this wonder.

Wonder it was, for scarce had we stepped from beneath the marquee into the street when the object came into view. How shall I describe this marvel? In length, it was perhaps an hundred and a half feet; shaped somewhat like a cigar, the two ends tapering to a rounded termination, it was, I should judge, some 25 to 30 feet in diameter through the central portion, and perhaps ten at the ends. The whole was constructed of some silvery metal which gave off an unearthly reddish glow, as if heated from within, as it hung motionless in the sky. As it floated over the town, it gave off a strange humming sound, unlike anything I had heard before. It was as if the player had held down the highest key and the lowest pedal on a pipe organ, but of an odd, almost frightening sonority.

For some full quarter hour by the town clock this strange object hung in the sky over the center of town, though a stiff breeze was blowing from the west, setting the flags in front of the new courthouse streaming as stiffly as if they had been dipped in starch.

But the most astonishing thing about the strange and wondrous object was that it was quite obviously inhabited. All along the forward — as we supposed, and would prove to be so — section of the object, or craft, we could clearly see a long row of round windows, with a yellowish glow showing through them, and here and there occluded by the head and shoulders of one of the occupants. At the center of the craft, along the upper surface, there appeared to be some sort of depression in which an external gallery had been set, and within which five of the inhabitants were promenading in order, I suppose, to observe we townsfolk even as we were, in our turn, observing them.

Now if the craft was astonishing in all respects, these occupants were yet more so. Borrowing a pair of field glasses from Mr. Carrington, I was able to observe the creatures — for I cannot call them men — with singular clarity. Their form was like to a man, but their bodies, which appeared to be entirely unclothed, were covered with scales, as if the serpent of old Eden was here appearing in his original form, before God deprived him of his limbs. In color, they were predominantly a rich, lustrous green, but the larger scales on their chests were a cream color. I can but suppose they found us quite as exotic as we found them, for they were continually pointing and, I suppose, conversing excitedly amongst themselves, though we could not hear them clearly enough over the sound of their craft to distinguish words, which I suppose we would not, in any case, have understood.

Whence came this weird craft and its reptilian inhabitants? From what part of the world? Young Master Donnelly was heard to speculate that it came not from some remote part of this world, but from some other world. The notion was quite rightly put down by the Reverend Mr. Morton, who firmly reminded the child that God had created life here alone, and reminded any who would think these creatures to be real that intelligence was limited to human beings, and had not been given to any other creatures, so it naturally followed that, whatever might appear to be the case, these "creatures" were without doubt men got up in outlandish costumes. As to what power was keeping the craft in the sky, the reverend gentleman was unwilling to speculate.

At length, the creatures promenading upon the upper gallery returned to the interior of their strange craft, which then rose vertically into the sky to a height of several hundred feet, after which it flew off toward the north at an astonishing speed, vanishing from sight in no more than a minute.

The newspaper was not, it should be stated, the only evidence of this remarkable event. Curtis Donnelly, the young Master Donnelly of the newspaper story, lived until 1924, and told the story to anyone who would listen, even writing a book, *The Collinsville Space Creatures*, in 1907. "I had to agree with the preacher at the time," he wrote, "being a kid and knowing full well that if I disagreed with him I'd get a good thrashing for my trouble. But I'm older now, and don't have to worry about that sort of thing, so I'm back to my original notion, which is that those creatures were from some other planet. Mars, maybe, even if they didn't look anything like what Mr. Wells wrote in his novel."

Unfortunately, no photographs were taken of the object. There was a photographer in Collinsville at the time, but by the time he was notified of what was happening and had brought out his equipment it proved too late to capture an image. According to the photographer's records, the craft flew off less than a minute after he had set up his camera, much too soon given that the slow emulsion on his photographic plates required an exposure of about eight minutes. So the only depiction of the craft was a woodcut that accompanied the newspaper article, and which has since been lost.

That this was a genuine sighting cannot be doubted, for the same strange craft was seen in a number of towns during the course of that day. Moreover, we have reports from some of those who were there, through the good offices of Dr. Jerold, who has discovered methods of communicating with the departed.

Dr. William Jerold, MD, a New York psychiatrist and hypnotherapist, has discovered that reincarnated spirits retain all of their former personalities and memories, but that these are normally suppressed, so that the body the spirit inhabits is unaware of this. Through hypnosis, these earlier incarnations can be contacted.

"The former personalities are distinct," Dr. Jerold relates. "They are all there, but never seem to be aware of each other, nor of the current incarnation, unless you give them the information. Also, spirits don't move around very much from one incarnation to the next, usually entering their next body within a few miles of where they died. Provided that the body doesn't move, it's not unusual to find that the spirit has lived in the same town for quite a long time.

"That's not to say that a soul that started out somewhere around Athens in Aristotle's time may not now be residing in Seattle. Spirits don't move very much, but people do, and they take their spirits with them. The limited mobility is only when the spirit is moving from its recently deceased host into a new body—usually, though not always, a newborn baby."

Recently, Dr. Jerold made contact with the personality of Reverend Jeremiah Morton, who was pastor of the Collinsville Methodist Church in 1847. Rev. Morton's spirit still resides in Collinsville or, at least, where Collinsville was formerly located, the village having long since been swallowed by Chicago. According to Dr. Jerold's research, Morton was the fourteenth incarnation of a spirit that had originated in 11th century England, and currently resides in a young Reform rabbi named Arnold Rothberg. This last incarnation, when revealed to Rev. Morton, brought a definite reaction, as recorded in this transcription of the interview.

Rev. Morton: You're telling me I'm living in a Jew now?

Dr. Jerold: Correct.

Rev. Morton: And I've been reincarnated? Into this Jew?

Dr. Jerold: Currently. With three other people in between.

Rev. Morton: So, reincarnation? You're telling me the goddamn *Hindus* were right?

Dr. Jerold: I suppose you could look at it that way if you wanted to, but that's not why I've brought you here.

Rev. Morton: What is?

Dr. Jerold: The UFO in Collinsville in 1847.

Rev. Morton: The what?

Dr. Jerold: The UFO. Unidentified flying object. The big metal thing in the sky with the reptile men aboard it.

Rev. Morton: Oh. What about it?

Dr. Jerold: Well, we're naturally interested in your thoughts about it.

Rev. Morton: Well, it was certainly one of Reilly's better efforts. I thoroughly enjoyed it.

Dr. Jerold: You enjoyed seeing the craft?

Rev. Morton: No, I enjoyed reading the story.

Dr. Jerold: What about the craft itself? What did that look like?

Rev. Morton: I never saw it. No one did. Reilly made it up.

Dr. Jerold: Are you saying this wasn't real?

Rev. Morton: Of course it wasn't real. What sort of idiot would think anything like that could really happen?

Dr. Jerold: Curtis Donnelly wrote a book about it.

Rev. Morton: Well, as I said, an idiot. I would wager he waited until most of the people who could dispute his story had died, didn't he?

Dr. Jerold: 1907.

Rev. Morton: I was gone by then. I remember dying at Gettysburg, which I thought was terribly unfair. After all, I was a chaplain, not a soldier, and not close to the fighting. Just bad luck. You're not supposed to fire artillery at the chaplain's tent.

Ultimately, it may be impossible to say with certainty what happened on that day in 1847. The newspaper article, along with Donnelly's book, seem to provide clear evidence that an object actually did hover over the town on that long ago day. The story told by Reverend Morton's reincarnated spirit disagrees, seeming to put the whole thing down to a newspaper editor who needed to fill some space and just made up a story. But who could believe that would ever happen?

We plan to continue our investigation.

CONFLICT OF INTEREST

Now I'm sure you can see, Susan, how important it is to get these books out of the school libraries in our district," Pastor Williams said, leaning forward in his chair and nibbling one of the ginger snaps Susan Evans had brought out for his visit.

These books, which so aroused the ire of her pastor, were the six so-far available volumes of the *Harry Potter* series, and Pastor Williams was absolutely certain that, if they were left in the school libraries, the children of Ellenville would all soon be seduced into some sort of devil worship. Susan was a member of the Ellenville Second Baptist Church, and she was also a member of the School Board, which was probably the more important membership at the moment so far as her pastor was concerned. He wanted to be sure he had her vote when the question of banning the books came up.

"You know," he went on, "there was a girl over in Custis who read all of the books over and over, and the next thing you know she was out in the woods with a bunch of witches, dancing naked around a bonfire, and worshipping Satan in some orgiastic rite. It was a terrible thing, really."

"I hadn't heard about that, Pastor."

"I learned of it from Reverend Zinser. He's a Methodist, but still a fine man. He was involved in getting her back from these New Age heathens. She's a good, born again Christian now, and has put this witchcraft behind her, and she's more than willing to speak to the School Board if it will help our cause."

"You know, Pastor," Susan said, "it sounds as if you're trying to use your position as my pastor to influence my vote."

"It's for a good cause. After all, you can't teach Christianity in the public schools—more's the pity—so why should you allow teachers to recommend books that teach this Wiccan nonsense?"

He's never read any of the books, Susan thought. "I'm not sure there are any Wiccans *in* those books," she said.

"Of course there are, Susan. They're full of witches, after all, and all witches are pagans."

"I always thought they were probably Church of England, mostly."

"Witches?"

"Well, the ones in those books. They're novels, after all. Children's stories, though I think most adults would enjoy them as well."

Pastor Williams took another ginger snap from the plate. He couldn't remember when he'd had anything so delicious, and for the moment he didn't care if he *was* cheating on his diet.

"You sound like you've read these books, Susan," he said.

"I have."

"Then you know what they're about. The sort of things that children are going to get out of them. Possibly be lured into."

"Honestly, Pastor, I think children are simply going to be entertained. And, like *Alice in Wonderland*, adults are going to find entirely different things. Just as a child is unlikely to recognize a satire on Victorian morality and society in *Alice*, he'd also be unlikely to see the parallels between the dark wizards and the Nazis. An adult would.

"But I don't think these are going to turn kids into witches any more than reading Superman comic books is going to give a kid the ability to fly. It's not presented as something you can learn, after all. It's presented as something that's inborn, and the only learning is how to control it. You can either do magic or you can't, but if you can you get to go to a boarding school to learn how to do it correctly."

"Well," Pastor Williams said, "the main thing is that we need to get these books out of the school libraries. One of the reasons we put so much effort into getting committed Christians onto the Board is so that we can do something about the atheistic and pagan influences the Liberals want to foist on our children."

"I'll have to think about it," Susan said.

As the pastor left, taking along a half dozen more ginger snaps, Susan wondered if God was really all that bothered by a series of children's books.

The opportunity to censor literature certainly wasn't why she had run for the School Board. It didn't even have that much to do with her being a Christian, though she had to admit that this had probably helped when it came to getting elected. Her concerns were really more for the fiscal policies of the school system, and a parent's suspicion that there were too many administrators and not enough actual educators.

She would think about her pastor's suggestion, but she didn't think it likely she'd vote the way he wanted. The books were actually pretty good, and it was hard enough to get kids to read these days without taking away books they liked.

Her consideration was interrupted by the sound of the back door opening, followed immediately by the refrigerator door opening, and the "pop" of a soda can. "I'm home, Mom," her son called.

Susan walked into the kitchen. "Where's your sister?"

"Cheerleader practice," Nick said.

"Oh." That was something else that Pastor Williams was, at best, ambiguous about. He was an ardent football fan, and regularly suggested that the congregation might want to spare a moment to remind God that the Ellenville Hornets deserved to win. But he also felt that the cheerleaders' uniforms were just a little too skimpy for good taste.

The fact was, Susan decided, the only things about the young witches and wizards in those books he would probably approve of were the English school uniforms they wore. Cover everything up, was his policy. Bare skin was bad.

"You have homework?" she asked.

"Yeah. I have to do a two page essay for English class."

"What about?"

Nick shrugged his shoulders. "Football, I think. You know, how a football team is a microcosm of society in general, and that sort of thing."

"Do you know what a microcosm is?" Susan asked.

"More or less. It sounds impressive, anyway, and I have to do two pages."

"Two pages isn't so bad."

"Yeah, Mom, but it's harder to do that now than when you were in school."

"You think so?"

"Sure. You guys wrote everything in longhand, didn't you? So if you needed to do two pages you just wrote big. Now we have to do this stuff on the computer and it takes a lot more words to fill two pages in 10 point Times New Roman."

"Nick, I'm not *that* old. We typed our essays, and your grandmother's typewriter had elite type, which isn't any bigger than what comes out of your printer."

Her son nodded and stuck his head back into the refrigerator. "Did I see the preacher leaving here just now, Mom?"

"Yes. He wants the School Board to ban *Harry Potter.*"

"Why?"

"He thinks the books promote devil worship or something."

"Now that's just silly."

"True. But our pastor is against them."

"That doesn't mean you have to go along with him, Mom."

"Well, you know, witches are all evil pagans, and it's up to us Christians to make sure that Satan doesn't get his claws into any more kids."

"He said that?"

"Yes."

"So are you going to vote the way he wants?"

"I have no idea. Probably not."

"Okay, then." Nick bit into an apple. "Anyway, I have to go write an essay."

Susan walked across the kitchen and took out a large pot. She figured spaghetti would be good for supper. She had her own recipe for the sauce, made from scratch. Fresh tomatoes, garlic, onions, olive oil, and a dozen Italian spices and a few other ingredients, several of which she refused to reveal to anyone. The complete recipe was locked up in the safe deposit box at the bank, and *might* be revealed to her daughter after she married.

Humming to herself, Susan started dicing an onion. She had barely begun when the fumes started to make her eyes water, so she walked into the living room, leaving the knife to continue working on the onions by itself.

She didn't think she would mention this particular food preparation technique to him, as it would certainly upset his world view, but, she decided, Pastor Williams would just have to understand if she didn't vote the way he wanted.

SKAGERRAK

Korvettenkapitän Hans Kruger glanced down at the circle of light from the open hatch at his feet. It was like the entrance to hell, glowing red from the night vision lights below. How many times, he wondered, had that literally been true for so many of his contemporaries? How many had entered the red-lit hull of a U-boat, only to find themselves minutes later facing eternity? It didn't bear thinking.

Kruger lifted his Zeiss glasses and scanned the dark horizon. *U-702* was surfaced, making good a steady 12 knots on her powerful diesels. On the deck, two of the engineering ratings were working in the dark, trying to repair the damage to the *Schnorchel* head.

It was too dangerous to be on the surface, even at night, Kruger knew. But with the *Schnorchel* damaged there was no choice. The batteries had to be charged, so they had surfaced after dark. If they could repair the *Schnorchel* while doing so, then they would submerge and continue charging in a slightly safer manner.

He glanced at the radar detector, mounted at the side of the bridge. It was the newest model; the engineers believed it would detect anything the Allies were using. But Kruger had heard those promises before. So had countless others, who had discovered the truth during their final moments of life.

Technology was a race. Once, before the war, the British had believed their Asdic had rendered the U-boat impotent as an offensive weapon. They had been wrong, but each advance in U-boat technology had shortly been followed by an advance in detection gear. As radar entered the picture, detectors had been fitted. But, again, the enemy was always upgrading their radar, learning to use ever shorter wavelengths, which both increased its accuracy and made it harder to detect.

Was their detector still useful, he wondered, or had the enemy already made it obsolete?

Behind him, the lookouts were carefully scanning their assigned sectors through powerful glasses. Where would the enemy be? Would the danger be on the surface, with enemy warships raining heavy shells on the fragile hull of the elderly submarine? Would their last moments be marked by the roar of aero engines, and the sudden, sun-like glare of a Leigh light? Or was there an enemy submarine lurking just under the surface, waiting quietly for them to cross her path before firing a torpedo?

Kruger frowned. *U-702's* tubes were empty, her last torpedo fired 12 days before. It had missed, but that miss had been followed by 78 hours of depth charging. There was the damage to the *Schnorchel*, and a British hedgehog mortar had broken the barrel off the deck gun. A lucky break, that one, Kruger thought, for had the mortar missed the gun it would have gone through the deck to explode against the pressure hull and *U-702's* career would have ended at the bottom of the North Atlantic, like so many of her sisters.

So now she was in the Skagerrak, steaming south, on her way back to Kiel, where she would undergo a complete refit. It would be a homecoming for the boat. She had been built in Kiel, two years earlier.

In the *Ubootwaffe*, *U-702* was considered a "lucky" boat. Kruger had commissioned her, just after his promotion to *Kapitänleutnant*. In the two years since, he had built up a tonnage record that rivaled the best of the early commanders, earning the Knight's Cross of the Iron Cross, with Oak Leaves and Swords, in the process.

During that time he had endured countless hours of slow, blind manoeuvring as the enemy escorts tried to kill him, yet he was still alive. More importantly, in those two years *U-702* had never lost a man, either to enemy action, or to accident or disease. The crew had become a perfectly-functioning team, seemingly able to read each other's thoughts. It was probably why they were all still alive.

His thoughts were interrupted by a sudden flash in the near distance. "Clear the bridge!" he shouted, his hand slamming against the red button under the screen. "Alarm!!!"

The two ratings who had been working on the *Schnorchel* came vaulting up onto the bridge as the lookouts tumbled down the hatch. Both knew that the captain cared for his crew as much as if they were his children, but he wouldn't risk the boat for anyone. If they didn't make it up to the bridge in time to get below they would have to swim for it and hope someone picked them up.

The boat was angling down, the sea rushing over her forecasing, even as Kruger dropped down the hatch, pulling it shut behind him and spinning the wheel. It had taken precious extra seconds to get the two engineering ratings below, but now they were under.

"Sixty metres," Kruger ordered, dropping down into the control room. "Steer two-seven-zero, revolutions for 3 knots."

He looked across the control room at the sound operator, who would have been monitoring the radar detector while they were surfaced. "No radar warning?"

The operator shook his head. "Nothing, sir. Never made a sound."

So the technology race, Kruger thought, had again shifted to the enemy. "What do you have, Krause?" he asked.

"Appears to be four contacts, about red nine-zero, and a fifth well beyond them. First four are on a converging course; fifth contact is steaming east."

Kruger nodded. There were reports of a British killer group operating in the Skagerrak. So the closest contacts, the ones closing on *U-702*, would be the anti-submarine ships—frigates, probably—and the more distant contact was most likely the carrier. In the dark, the frigates would be the real threat, for it was unlikely the carrier's planes would be risked except in an emergency. It was dangerous enough landing a plane at night at a proper airfield; it would be doubly so on the tiny deck of an escort carrier.

There had been no explosion, nor any sound of the enemy's shell striking the sea. So it had probably been a star shell. If it was still drifting beneath its parachute, it would be illuminating only empty sea. But the enemy had fired, and that almost certainly meant they had got a radar contact. They knew something had been there; that there was nothing now meant a submarine.

So the hunt would begin.

Beneath *U-702*'s keel, the hulks of old High Seas Fleet units lay together with their victims from the Grand Fleet. That had been a grand action, huge fleets of battleships and battle-cruisers manoeuvring for advantage in history's last great sea battle. Swift destroyers flanking their giant consorts, darting in to attack with their lighter guns and torpedoes.

Kruger's father had been there, as a junior gunnery officer in a battle-cruiser. He had survived, though his ship had not.

There was a soft sound coming from the hull, like someone running a metal brush against the casing.

Richter, the Exec, was at his side. "I hope they're not paying attention," he said.

"So do I, Number One," Kruger said. He knew better, but it was important to appear confident. The crew expected it.

Again, there was the metallic brushing sound, louder this time, and followed by the roar of a warship's screws as she rushed through the sea directly overhead.

"Full speed!" Kruger ordered. "Steer one-nine-zero!"

"Depth charges coming down!" the sound operator shouted, pulling off his padded earphones to avoid being deafened by the explosions.

U-702 swung around onto her new course, her speed creeping up to six knots as the e-motors wound up to full speed.

The stern lifted and slewed to port as the pattern detonated perhaps 30 metres astern, and slightly below, the boat.

"All stop! Damage report!"

Quickly, the reports came in from the sealed compartments. Nothing was leaking; no obvious damage reported.

For the next three hours, the rain of depth charges and hedgehog mortars was almost continuous. *U-702* would constantly change depth, sometimes sprinting as the enemy charged in for the attack, then sitting still as the enemy did the same, listening to determine if his depth charges had done their job. There had been so many course changes that Kruger had begun to lose track of their position, which was an added worry.

Above them, the four British frigates alternately attacked and listened. Their commander recognised the skill of his opponent. But he had a long string of victories to his credit, and was determined to add another. He knew he had the advantage. He could continue attacking for as long as it took. His intended victim could stay down only so long before running out of air, or exhausting his batteries. After that, he would be forced to surface or die.

By now, the air was beginning to go bad in the battered U-boat. Kruger remained by the plot table, calling course and depth changes as he reacted to the enemy's attacks. He couldn't even shoot back, with his tubes empty.

Another pattern exploded, much too close, throwing *U-702* violently off course. Something was banging against the casing, making a horrible racket.

"All stop."

The noise subsided as they slowed. The last pattern had clearly blasted something loose. The damage did not appear to be fatal, but the noise almost certainly would be. If they attempted to move, the banging would betray their position to the enemy. If they stayed still, it would be only a matter of time before the enemy pinned them down in their Asdic and destroyed them.

He could see it on the faces of the other men in the control room. A U-boat's most valuable defensive asset was silence. If the enemy couldn't hear you, he probably couldn't kill you.

Again, one of the enemy warships passed over the boat, the sound of her Asdic audible against the hull. But there were no depth charges. Had something malfunctioned? Kruger wondered.

"Enemy is breaking off," Krause reported.

"Why?" Richter wondered aloud.

"There's a lot of high speed HE, about green four-five," Krause reported. "Enemy are turning to intercept."

Kruger looked at the chart. That would put the new HE to the east. If the enemy frigates were turning toward it, it would mean friendly forces, coming out from Denmark.

"What do the newcomers sound like, Krause?"

"Very fast. Estimate about 40 knots, sir."

Kruger smiled. *Schnellboote*, then. They'd keep the enemy busy, perhaps even sink something. But the important thing was that they would give the British killer group something more immediate to worry about. Kruger had never shot back, so they had to at least suspect he was out of torpedoes. The S-boats would undoubtedly be fully armed.

"Enemy have increased speed and are engaging with guns," Krause reported. "They should be making too much noise to hear us now."

"Then we'll take advantage of it," Kruger said. "Steer one-eight-four. Revolutions for three knots."

Slowly, her damaged casing banging in the flow, *U-702* turned south and worked her way out of the danger zone. They had survived.

For now.

[The story of what happened after this is found in the novel *With Honour in Battle*, available in trade paperback, Kindle, and Nook versions from Riverdale Electronic Books.]

A BIG DISAPPOINTMENT

I've always been a good ball player. The first time I came up to bat in my first Little League game I knocked the ball over the left field fence. Well, that sort of thing happens. What was surprising was that I kept it up. Not hitting home runs every time I came to bat—no one does that, unless maybe they've got some guy named Applegate sitting in the stands cheering them on. But I've always hit better than average.

My senior year in high school I finished the season with a .358 average. When I wasn't swinging a bat I was out in right field. That doesn't mean I wasn't a good fielder, either. Our team had enough really good outfielders that they didn't have to put the weakest one in right field.

I got half a dozen scholarship offers from colleges wanting me to play on their teams. They were all tempting, a couple *very* tempting, because there was no way I was getting into an Ivy League school if we had to pay for it. But the offer from the Indians trumped anything Harvard could come up with. Even going into class A ball, I'd be making about as much as one of those Ivy League schools would charge for tuition. If I made it to Cleveland, even the league minimum would be enough that after four or five years I could expect to be pretty well set for life. And not that many people made the minimum.

That was one of those jokes most people missed in *Major League*. When Tom Berringer's character admits he just makes the league minimum, it sounds like he's just barely getting by. The crummy apartment he's sharing with Charlie Sheen's character adds to that impression. What he was actually saying, though, was that he was making a bit over $400,000 for the season. It's been a long time since major league players needed to sell cars in the off season.

Going with the Indians would also make my mother *really* happy. She's been a die-hard Indians fan just about forever. Oh, she'll grouse when they're not winning, but she's been going downtown a couple dozen times a season since she was a kid back in the 1960s. When I signed a development contract with the Indians you'd have thought Jesus had come back the way she was carrying on.

She's not real fond of me at the moment, though.

I made it to the big leagues this Spring. The problem, from Mom's perspective, is that I didn't make it to Cleveland.

Most of last year I spent in Columbus. The Clippers are Cleveland's AAA farm team, so the chances of moving up were good. My average was down a little since high school. It's a lot harder to stay in the middle .300s once you start facing professional pitching. But .293 is respectable enough these days. And I figured I was getting better and could expect to be moving up soon.

Then the leagues decided to expand again. I'm not entirely sure how it happened that Fort Myers got one of the new teams, but they did. Instead of heading up I-71 to Cleveland, I found myself going south to join the initial roster of the Fort Myers Cattlemen. The name of the team didn't make much sense to me, either. But apparently there are a lot of cows in Florida, and it seems that Fort Myers essentially started out as a cattle town.

Jimmy Vega, our manager, told me once I should probably be happy the owners picked the name they did. "The other thing this town was really known for was raising gladioluses," he explained. "You could have been playing for the Glads."

The fact that my mother was unhappy with where I ended up should probably tell you that Fort Myers was a new American League team. She could have tolerated it if I'd ended up in the National League, where I'd be a lot less likely to play against *her* team. Mind you, she'd still be getting annoyed during inter-league play, but who doesn't?

I don't think anybody likes inter-league games, except maybe the owners. Most of them like baseball, I'm sure, but they like money more. That's the only way I can explain playoffs. I suppose I can understand the idea for pro football. They don't play that many games, so it's not that unlikely to end up with a five way tie for first place at the end of the season. But that's not the case with baseball. We play 162 games every year. That cuts way down on the number of ties, though it doesn't eliminate them entirely.

Well, that's why we keep track of errors, isn't it? If you get to the end of the season and you have three teams with identical win-loss records, you can look at the errors to see which one screwed up the least. Doing it that way avoids idiotic situations like the 1996 World Series, where the National League was represented by the Atlanta Braves, who had finished the season in first place and survived the playoffs. The American league, however, was represented by the Yankees, who finished the season with a 97-70 record, instead of the Indians, who finished with a 99-62 record. Why was the second place team in the Series? Because the Orioles got lucky in the playoffs and knocked Cleveland out of contention.

With the old system, Cleveland would have been in the Series. Whether they would have beat Atlanta I'm not going to guess.

Why are there playoffs when you don't really need them? Money. Adding playoffs gives the owners of the teams that are in them the chance to sell tickets to all those extra games. Owners like money. You can't really blame them. I like money, too. But I'd still rather see the league championships decided the old-fashioned way, by the regular season records.

Come to think of it, the '96 season was the last one where I can remember newspapers routinely printing the overall league standings during the regular season. I can't help wondering if someone in the Commissioner's office told them to cut that out so it wouldn't be so obvious if that sort of travesty happened again.

When the opportunity to go to Fort Myers was presented, I naturally took it. The alternative wasn't staying in Columbus, after all, it was trying to find a job in Mexico or Japan. The league wasn't going to let anyone duck out of this one.

I told Mom that it probably didn't matter all that much. "What kind of chance do you think an expansion team has of accomplishing anything in its first season?" I asked.

"You never know. I'm getting old, and the Indians don't seem to be playing any better than they ever did."

"Well, maybe this year." I was being optimistic. The Indians had done pretty good back in the '90s. Having Hollywood make fun of them, and then moving to a new ballpark, had really brought the team to life.

The last few years, though, they've gone back to being themselves. They still have a better record than the Cubs, but that's not saying very much. Everybody has a better record than the Cubs.

So did we, as it turned out.

Our first regular season game was on the road against New York. No pressure there, huh? Take a brand new team and start them out against the current world champions.

We'd done okay in the pre-season games. Not spectacular, but okay. The league had been kinder to us there. Mostly, the new teams played each other, with just a handful of games against the established teams. The thing about pre-season games is they don't count. It's all practice, really, though the fans tend to take it seriously.

After the National Anthem had been sung, and the home plate umpire had yelled, "Play ball!" my first question was whether I'd bat in this inning. I was fourth in the lineup, after Murphy, Carasco, and Lovett. Jimmy Vega was telling us we'd get through the whole lineup at least twice in the first inning. We figured we'd be doing okay if the Yankees didn't strike out all of us in order and get themselves a no hitter.

Jim Murphy was one of the veterans from the expansion draft. He'd played three seasons with Pittsburgh, and came with a .265 batting average. Obviously, no one had put their best players in the draft, but he was at least used to major league pitching, so that put him one up on me. I was used to AAA pitching. Almost the same thing, but not all AAA pitchers move up to the big team, so sometimes you're facing major league pitching, and sometimes you're facing *almost* major league pitching. Almost is easier to hit.

Murphy bats right handed. He faced that first pitch like a veteran. He watched it whisk past him like a veteran, too. This is a good thing. It was a ball. Well, I thought, this is a good start.

He misjudged the next one. The ball blazed past, but this time the umpire decided it was in the strike zone. So, one and one.

He swung at the next ball, which went straight up and back. Carillo, the Yankees catcher, threw off his mask and hurried back to get under the ball. We lucked out. The ball hit the top of the net and went into the stands. That made the count one and two. Time to knock the ball out of the park, I thought, because I didn't think Gonzalez was going to suddenly decide to throw three more balls. In five seasons with the Yankees, Gonzalez had a bad habit of striking people out on a regular basis.

Swing and a miss. So much for Murphy.

Julio Carasco was up next. Catchers are often good hitters, and Carasco was no exception, with a .305 average. He seemed like a nice enough guy, not that we'd ever had much chance to talk about anything. Julio could just about manage to keep from starving in English. No problem for Jimmy Vega, who spoke the Puerto Rican Spanish he'd picked up in his parents' home in the Bronx. I grew up in Bedford, one of the southeast Cleveland suburbs, where you didn't have that many Spanish speakers. My parents insisted I take a language in high school, but I took German.

Spanish probably would have been more useful.

Better timing might have been useful to Julio. He struck out on the first three pitches. My chances of batting in the first inning depended on Lovett now. If he didn't hit safely, or at least walk, I'd be heading out to my place in right field before long.

Lovett was a hell of a guy. With the count three and two he connected with a curve ball, sending it screaming just over the shortstop's head and deep into left field. He crossed first base about the same time the left fielder ran over and picked up the ball. So we had one man on base and it was time for me to make my major league debut.

The first pitch was a fastball. I figured it was going to be in the strike zone, so I swung the bat, catching it low and bouncing it down the wrong side of the first base line. Oh and one.

Gonzales decided to be consistent. He threw the same pitch, but this time I caught it square and the ball went soaring out into right field. Guerra was out of position, made a frantic leap, and the ball looked as if it may have actually touched his glove before taking off past him and rolling across the warning track to come to rest against the fence.

Lovett had made it to second base before I was halfway to first. Guerra was still trying to recover the ball as my foot hit the base, so I made the turn and Lovett continued on to third.

Over at third base, Carl Zworkin had one eye on Guerra and was frantically waving Lovett around third and simultaneously waving me on. Guerra had the ball now and hesitated maybe half a second before throwing the ball to second. There was no way he could get the ball to third in time to beat me, so the logical choice was to hope he could get it to second and make the relay to home before Lovett could get there.

There wasn't much chance of that. Lovett was across home plate before the ball was past the mound. I stayed on third.

Michaels got a single, and that got me home. Then Gomez flied out. I grabbed my glove and headed for the outfield.

The Yankees won that game, but we made them work for it. The final score was Yankees 8, Cattlemen 7. They won it with a two-run homer in the bottom of the ninth. The next day we got back at them, taking a three run lead in the sixth inning and then holding them scoreless for the rest of the game. Final score on the second game, Yankees 5, Cattlemen 8.

About a third of the way into the season the sportswriters were allowing as to how we were doing really well for an expansion team. The other new teams, Las Vegas and Birmingham in the AL, and New Orleans, Chattanooga, and Honolulu in the NL, weren't doing as well.

Vegas had the best ballpark, a 53,000 seat domed setup that was kept at a nice, even 75° on game days. It was the only one of the new ballparks that was under cover, but you had to remember that a lot of times the outside temperature would be something like 118°, and no one wanted to watch a lot of baseball players dropping dead of heat stroke if they had to chase after a fly.

The Vegas owners were somewhat saddened when the league nixed their plans to include a couple thousand slot machines and a sports book into the place. The league said they would just have to make do with ticket sales, TV money, and merchandising, like everyone else. I guess the owners somewhat compensated by working in the leagues first triple-deck luxury box setup. You had your normal seats around the field, then three tiers of luxury boxes, then the upper deck. Just to be thorough, they also slipped in ten field level luxury boxes, five on either side of home plate.

The box owners could decorate them any way they wanted, so a few poker tables and slots still managed to make their way into the place. They just weren't accessible to the general public.

Honolulu was where we all wanted to play away games. Their 42,000 seat ballpark was really nice, but it was where it was located that made us want to play there. Being on the road staying in a beachfront hotel in Honolulu just beats the hell out of what you get at a road game in, say, Detroit, where you often wonder if it wouldn't be a good idea to commute between Comerica Park and your hotel in an armored car.

The first game my mother attended was when we played a four game series in Cleveland in early May. She was just barely willing to talk to me after it was over. She could tolerate the fact that Cleveland lost, but it annoyed the hell out of her that it was my home run in the eighth that clinched the game for Fort Myers.

Cleveland was actually doing pretty good this year. They were first in the AL Central division, and only one game behind the Yankees in the overall record on the season. We were second in the AL East, two games behind the Yankees. Us winning this game left Cleveland still in sole possession of first in the Central division, but dropped them back one game on the overall record. It didn't move us up any, since the Yankees won their game that day.

The game had been played on Sunday, so we played in the afternoon. It was good to be home, even if I'd come home as the "enemy." It was also nice to be playing in a ballpark with a traditional name. At the beginning of the season a rich guy from Shaker Heights had put up a huge amount of money to buy the naming rights from Progressive, and had promptly given the ballpark its third name. Originally it had been Jacobs Field, after the team's old owner. Then it had been Progressive Field, though a lot of people continued to refer to the place as "the Jake" for the whole Progressive period. The guy from Shaker Heights—part of the deal was that no one was allowed to say who he was—had decided that thereafter the place would be called New League Park. Whoever he was, I liked him.

I liked tradition, too. All that was left of the original League Park was part of one wall. And maybe the new name was helping, because the Indians hadn't played that good in quite a few years.

Down in Fort Myers, we played our home games in Best Buy-Florida Citrus Park, and while we were the Fort Myers Cattlemen, the ballpark was actually located in northern Cape Coral, on the other side of the river.

By the All Star break, Fort Myers was solidly in possession of first place in the AL East, with a five game lead on New York. Cleveland was still first in the AL Central, though only by two games, and my mother wasn't talking to me at all. If I called home it was always my Dad who answered. He liked baseball, but it wasn't a religion for him and as long as it was a good game he didn't really care who won.

"Why is it," I asked, "that every time I call home you always answer? You'd think once in a while Mom would pick up the phone by accident."

"Caller ID," Dad said. "She sees your name, points at me, and says, 'It's for you'." He paused for a moment. "Your stats look pretty good, Ed," he added.

I had pushed my average up to .347 by now, and had 31 home runs. I didn't think I was any threat to Babe Ruth, but I was doing more than okay for a rookie. "I just wish Mom was happier about it," I said.

"Oh, she's happy enough. She's just pissed you're doing it for a team that could wind up in the playoffs with the Indians and maybe keep us out of the Series for another year. The Tribe's playing really good this season.

Remember, your Mom was born in 1948, and that was the last time the Indians won the Series. She was too young for that one and she wants to see them win another one."

"You don't really think we're going to make it to the Series this year, do you, Dad?"

"I know you're going to try."

We did, too. And come fall the Cattlemen were firmly in possession of first place in our division, as was Cleveland in theirs. In the first series, Cleveland would take on Oakland, the wild card, and we would play Detroit. Both series went the full five games, and when it was all over Mom's fears were realized. Cleveland would play Fort Myers for the league championship, and her son was in a position to destroy her dreams for another year at least.

You could argue that Cleveland was slightly the better team. Under the old system they'd have gone into the World Series at the end of the regular season with a 95-67 record. We would have been in second place with 94-68. What this meant under the current system was that the first two games would be played in Cleveland.

Grantland Rice couldn't have done much with the sky as we lined up along the first base line for the National Anthem. October it might have been, but there wasn't a cloud to be seen. "Under a bright blue October sky" just doesn't have the same ring.

We took the first game 6-3. I hit a solo home run in the ninth inning, which would be the final run scored in that game. I came around third base heading for home to the sight of my mother, sitting in the first row behind the Indians' dugout, shaking her fist at me with a weak smile on her face. It can't be easy to have a kid excel at something you love, but do it for the enemy.

The Indians got back into things in the second game. Our left fielder, Nick Burton, got a home run in the second inning and that was it for us. It really looked like it would be enough, because it was still 1-0 Cattlemen in the ninth inning. But the Indians got two runs in the bottom of the ninth, so the series was tied up 1-1 and it was time to head south for the next three games.

I can tell you that both teams were hoping that the next three games would be all we had to play. We liked the idea that we would be playing them at home.

It started off good. We took the next two games 10-8 and 3-1. Then the Indians came back to take the last game in Fort Myers 8-7 in 14 innings. So we would have to play at least one more game, maybe two. We were hoping for one, the Indians were hoping for two with them winning both. We'd play them in their ballpark, something that was more likely to help them than us.

It did, too. They took the next game 9-4. There is probably no moment in the life of a professional baseball player to compare with the sight of your own mother leaping up and down in sheer joy as she watches you get tagged out at third. That was the end of the game.

The next would decide it.

My father invited me out to the house for lunch the next day, but I decided to remain at the hotel downtown and eat with the team. Jimmy told me he didn't care if I went out to Bedford, since I was from there. "I'd rather stay here," I said. "I love my mother, but I wouldn't put it past her to spike the potato salad with salmonella to keep me from playing tonight."

I'm still not entirely sure I was joking.

Some writer sang the national anthem. This was actually a little refreshing, because the old guy sang it straight and didn't have to cheat on the high notes. After that one of the local TV sports guys got to throw the ceremonial first pitch. The sports guy had played football in college, not baseball, so he threw the ball from about the midway point between home plate and the mound and put the ball about four feet to the left of the strike zone even from there. I could remember sitting in the stands once and watching Bob Feller throw a first pitch from about the same location, but Feller was over 90 at the time, and even if he couldn't throw as far any more he still got it over the plate.

As we were playing the final game in Cleveland, we were up first. I've never been sure which is better. The visiting team always has the first chance to score, but the home team finishes the game and gets the final chance to catch up and win.

I don't know what Jim Murphy thought about that, but he knocked the first pitch out into right field, where it proceeded to bounce over the fence. Murphy started running as the ball came off the bat, but he slowed to a fast jog once the ball was gone. He was going to second base and there was no particular hurry getting there now. From where I was sitting in the dugout, the significance of this was mostly that I'd be batting in the first inning.

Carasco singled on the second pitch, but Murphy was blocked from advancing. We had two men on base and Lovett was looking for a chance to get them home. Instead he got nowhere, swinging and missing at the first three pitches.

My turn.

As I was taking my practice swings and hoping Lovett would get a hit and load up the bases for me, I looked over behind the Indians' dugout, where my mother was sitting in her full outfit of Indians home jersey and a late 1950s cap, holding what looked like my old high school fielder's glove. If I didn't know for sure that he was dead I'd have sworn Ray Walston was sitting next to her. That's the sort of thing that can throw you. I couldn't really see her making some sort of deal with the devil even to insure the Indians made it into the series, but the old guy sitting next to her did give that impression.

I probably watch too many old movies. I didn't see Gwen Verdon or Tab

Hunter around, anyway, so I just put it down to an over-active imagination and took a few more swings.

I took six more swings at the plate, not that it helped much. One strike, four consecutive foul balls, and another strike. The last foul should have been good for a base hit; the ball couldn't have missed the foul side of the post by more than a quarter inch. If it had managed to actually *hit* the post, ground rules would have called it a home run.

After I missed the last pitch, Mom was on her feet applauding. I love my mother, but this year has definitely tested that affection.

For this inning, at least, me striking out didn't matter that much. Michaels got hold of the second pitch and sent it onto the home run porch beyond the left field fence. That brought Murphy and Carasco home, making the score 3-0 Fort Myers with two outs.

Gomez kept it going with a single that went between Begun's legs and rolled off into left field. By the time Begun could spin around and chase down the ball Gomez had crossed first and Cleveland's shortstop was left holding the ball. He threw it to Kaminski behind the plate, who handed it to the umpire and got a new ball for Elvin to pitch to Yamada.

Yamada, our designated hitter, was another one who was hard to talk to. He spoke English, but he spoke it the way they teach it in Japan. They tell me this is what you get when a language is taught by people who learned it from other people who were also not native speakers. You get Japanese vowels and consonants, and it seems as if just about every other word ends with a "U." We could all understand his favorite phrase, though: "Ho-mu rah-nu."

Which he did not get this time, but not for a lack of trying. Collins caught the ball right at the fence in far right field. It was almost as hard to imagine as that ridiculous backwards catch of Mays during the '54 Series.

I passed Yamada as he was coming back to the dugout, shaking the jagged handle of his bat. The fat part had come close to clobbering the bat boy, and just about everyone agreed that the ball would have gone over the fence if the bat hadn't broken. Yamada was muttering something in Japanese, and I heard Jimmy asking him what he was saying.

"No mo fukingu maapu!" Yamada declared.

I quite agreed. Call me a traditionalist, but I haven't used a maple bat since my first year in the minors. A lot of players like them, but the damn things break too easy. I stick to the old ash bats, and get them in Louisville. This first year in the majors I've hit good enough that the Ed Johnson signature bat started coming out of the Louisville Slugger plant in August.

Our starter, Diego Estancia, threw his practice pitches to Carasco, then waited for the first batter. It was the sort of performance you always want to see, but almost never do. Collins was called out without ever swinging the bat. Martinez swung and missed three times in a row, and Kaminski swung and missed twice and then took a called strike to end the inning. The inning lasted 18 minutes; the Indians were up for the last six. Estancia came back to the dugout looking remarkably refreshed, which I suppose made sense, considering he'd only thrown nine pitches.

In the second, things were more or less reversed. Carillo didn't manage a nine pitch inning against us, but five singles didn't manage to get a single player home before the side was retired and the Indians were up again.

Estancia fanned Archie Dunstan, the Indians first baseman. But then Begun came up to redeem his screwed up fielding with a triple, and their DH, Oliver, knocked a home run over the center field fence. So now it was 3-2 Fort Myers, and one out in the bottom of the second.

Third baseman John Borden was next in the lineup. He was new to the Indians this season, and I knew him fairly well, having played with him in Columbus last year. I went with my experience, which was to play well back in right field. Borden reminded me of Baerga back in his days with Cleveland. He hit a lot of foul balls, but if once he connected with something that would stay fair the ball tended to travel.

I was half right. After five consecutive foul balls Borden connected and sent the ball soaring in my direction. As it turned out, I wasn't quite far enough back in right field. If I wanted to catch that one I should have been standing next to a hot dog vendor about ten rows back in the stands. So now the game was tied in the second inning, and still only one out for the Indians.

And that was where the score stayed. Both teams put up lots of hits in the following innings, but when we came up in the top of the ninth it was still 3-3.

I had my doubts that I'd bat again in this game. We were down near the bottom of the lineup, with our left fielder, Nick Burton, up first. Burton batted eighth, and I batted fourth, so including Burton there were five players between me and my next chance at bat. I figured my next time up to the plate would be if we went into extra innings, which seemed fairly likely with the score still tied.

Burton worked up to a full count before swinging at a slider from Indians closer Paul Lejeune. My mother hated LeJeune, and was known to argue that when it came to him "closer" was spelled wrong—the first letter didn't belong there. She probably wasn't complaining at the moment, though.

Rick Almadovar was up next, about to hit into what every commentator in baseball would soon be calling the single worst fielding display of the season. With two strikes and no balls, he leveled the bat and bunted. The ball hit the ground about ten feet in front of the plate, and Kaminski was after it like a shot.

Or maybe more like a shot put. In going after the ball he tripped over the plate and by the time he recovered and had his hands on the ball Almadovar was past first and on his way to second.

Kaminski threw the ball to Steadman at second. At least, he tried to. Maybe he was still a little off from tripping, because the ball went over Steadman's head, and Loring and Martinez were running in to grab it before any more damage could be done.

Meanwhile, Carl Zworkin was waving Almadovar around. Loring got the ball, but Almadovar beat it to third base by about four seconds. More than that, really, because Borden dropped the thing. From the front of the dugout you could almost see Zworkin and Almadovar thinking it might just be worth it to try for home. But fast as Almadovar was—I've seen him run the hundred in nine flat—they both recognized that Borden wouldn't have to do much more than bend over to grab the ball and throw it home, and there was no way they could count on Kaminski screwing up again.

By the time it was all over I still wasn't quite sure what I'd seen. Not only the horrible fielding, but there was the question of why Almadovar had bunted with no one on base. The odds were against him even getting a single out of it, much less making it all the way to third.

As it turned out, I didn't have that long to wait to find out what he'd been thinking. Murphy came up next and hit a single on the first pitch, bringing Almadovar home. More bad fielding on the part of the Indians accomplished this. Murphy hit almost directly to Borden, who let his instincts override his common sense. Instead of letting Murphy have the base hit and throwing the ball to home to cut off what was potentially the game-winning run, Borden threw to first. Murphy beat the throw by maybe half a second.

That made it 4-3 Fort Myers, with only one out.

"What the hell were you thinking?" Jimmy asked Almadovar, when he was back in the dugout. "It worked, but why the hell did you bunt?"

Rick was swinging his right forearm in a tight circle. "Desperation, *jefé*. I think maybe I pulled something on that second swing. It was either try for a bunt, or hope Lejeune would decide to throw four balls. I figured the odds were better with the bunt." He grinned. "Of course, I didn't really figure they would be as good as they turned out."

But that was it for us. Carasco struck out, and Lovett sent a fly ball deep into center field, where Loring caught it easily.

Well, I thought, as I took my place in right field, now we have to work against the home field advantage. We were ahead, but the Indians were up again and had a chance to either tie it up again, or win outright. The notion that a first-year expansion team appeared ready to take away a chance at a world championship was likely to be pretty motivating.

Kaminski was up first. He let one strike go by, then a ball. On the next pitch he swung hard, sending the ball out on a line to me. I was playing back and the ball hit the ground as I was running in. I had it before it could even bounce, but Kaminski was at first before the ball got there.

Dunstan struck out. Then Mike Welsh walked Begun and Oliver, loading up the bases. I figured Mom was probably fairly happy about now. Borden could hit, and Welsh could hardly throw around him, because that would walk in the tying run and set up Steadman to knock in the game winner.

Welsh tossed a 96 mile an hour fastball right over the plate and Borden connected with a solid hit right back at the pitcher's mound.

Welsh took a half step to the right and scooped it up as it bounced up the front of the mound. Unlike Borden in the top of the inning, Welsh knew which player was more important at the moment. He had the ball back to Carasco before Kaminski was halfway home. That made it two outs, but the bases were still loaded.

That brought up Curt Steadman, the second baseman. He was another Indian we had to respect, coming into the game with a .337 average, 38 home runs on the season, and two more in the playoffs.

The first pitch was a fastball, swung on and missed. The next two were balls. From where I was standing I could see the Indians manager looking hopeful. A base hit would tie it up, a double or better would win it. Even a walk would get them a tie and another chance to win it if they couldn't in this inning.

Steadman swung on the next pitch and knocked a high screamer toward right field. Dunstan was heading for home. I was running in, not really thinking about what I was doing. Somewhere down in the primitive part of my brain something knew where the ball was going and I needed to get there first.

The ball dropped neatly into my glove about four seconds before Dunstan made it home. Four seconds was enough, though. The game was already over when he got there.

We were going to the World Series.

I figured it might be safe to go home again sometime after the Super Bowl. But only if the Browns managed to win it.

MEMOIR

I had a different name when I was young. My parents named me Septimus Morenus Altimanus. Septimus, which means seventh, suggests to me that, like many Romans, they simply got tired of thinking up names for their children and started numbering us instead. We were Marcus, Horatius, Drusilla, Brutus, Quintus, Sextus, Septimus, and Octavius, so the first four, including my sister, had real names and the rest of us were numbered.

I was born on the fifth day of October, in what would now be considered 72 BCE, in Herculaneum. On today's calendar that would be August fifth, as this was before Julius and Augustus Cæsar inserted themselves into the calendar, shifting the last four months further back. Given that the last four were numbered, confusion has reigned ever since. This is how it happens that the twelfth month in the year, December, means "tenth month." You probably found this sort of thing annoying in Latin class, presuming you took it.

I did, of course, but when I was born that's what we spoke, so it was a lot easier. There was no translating to worry about, for one thing. I *did* have to study Greek, but we also commonly spoke that. We Romans were something like the Russians of the early 19th century. Just as they found it somehow more fashionable to speak French in society rather than their own language, so educated Romans made a point of speaking Greek.

Because I was seventh born, and the sixth son of a remarkably healthy family, there was little chance that I would ever inherit more than the few personal items my father might wish me to have. The bulk of the estate would go to my brother Marcus. It was therefore decided that I would go into the army.

My father was a senator, which gave him a certain amount of interest. By the time I was 20 I had been commissioned as centurion, and placed in command of a century in the 14th Legion. The name suggests that I commanded 100 troops, but it was actually 80 combat troops, and another 20 administrative types. Even then the number of non-combatants needed to support the actual fighters was growing.

In the Spring of 47 BCE our legion was sent into Thrace to put down a rebellion. That was when things changed, in the midst of a small battle, involving only my own century against a little band of Thracian infantry. During the fight I was wounded by a spear thrust to my right thigh.

It was not, in itself, a serious wound. The iron point didn't so much penetrate as slice, laying open the skin for a length of perhaps two inches, and only slightly damaging the muscle beneath. But there was always a danger of infection in those days, long before anyone had ever heard of antibiotics. Within a few days the wound began to fester.

That was when Meskhenet appeared. She was one of the women who followed in the wake of our army. No one was entirely sure of where she came from, though her name was clearly Egyptian. There was even a question of why she was there. She wasn't a prostitute, nor was she a cook, or a laundress. Sometimes she would sit with the injured, and sometimes they would get well and sometimes they wouldn't. Perhaps two of ten whom she watched over would be healed, and if that doesn't sound particularly impressive, remember that most physicians did little better and many did less well.

The first time she came into my tent she ejected everyone else, sat by my cot, took my hand in hers, and told me that she could certainly heal me, and even save my infected leg—which our physician wanted to cut off—but that there would be a price.

"What price?" I asked. My father was rich, and would certainly pay well to keep any of his children in health.

"Not money," she explained. "My price is more personal."

"In what way?"

"If I heal you, you will be healthy in the future, but you also be different. You will gain not only the few years you might normally expect, but many more as well."

"How many?"

"Perhaps only a few, perhaps hundreds, perhaps thousands."

"What are you, a goddess offering immortality?"

"No. Many would go so far as to call me accursed, even a demon. I am not. In most ways I am quite ordinary, a woman with all the virtues and faults of any other woman, except that I have lived much longer than anyone you have ever known."

She looked to be but little past twenty.

"But you must know that if you are healed, the day will almost surely come when your friends denounce you. When they are old and you are still young. When their children are old and you are still young." She smiled. "And, you must know, you will take no pleasure in the foods you now love, nor will they nourish you. You will live only on blood."

It was a curious idea. Live on blood?

"Human blood?"

"Any blood will nourish—but human tastes best."

"You're a vampire?"

She nodded her head. "As I said, I like you, Septimus. It is only because of this that I offer you this chance. It will hurt far less than you think. I will merely take a little of your blood, hardly more than a thimble-full each time. Each day for a fortnight I will do this, and at the end of that time you will be healed, but you will also be as I am, a drinker of blood, a vampire."

The worst part was that I had to make the choice at once. I did not have the option to think about it for a few days, because in a few days the infection would kill me.

"How old are you, exactly?" I asked.

"I was born in Egypt, in the same year that the Israelites departed our country amidst horrendous plagues. I never knew my father, for he was a first born, and so he died shortly before I was born, along with all the others."

I knew enough of this Jewish story to know that it had supposedly happened centuries ago. Was it possible that this girl was truly immortal?

Still, there was not much of a choice. The worst that could happen was that I would die, something the physicians had determined was almost certainly inevitable. It was a choice between possible immortality and death. Not much of a choice, I thought.

I said, "Yes."

There was almost no pain. Meskhenet's canine teeth sank into my shoulder. She made no attempt to puncture an artery; the blood that welled up from the ruptured capillaries in the skin and muscle was sufficient to her purpose. And, as she had said, she returned to my tent each day for the next two weeks, each day taking a little more blood.

And each day the infection in my leg relented, and my health improved. As she had predicted, my hunger for normal foods diminished as my strength returned. I began to crave blood, and this Meskhenet supplied, bringing it to me in a wine bottle. She said that it came from a cow.

In recent years I have concluded that the transmission of vampirism is the result of a virus injected by the bite. It is not a particularly virulent virus, and requires repeated exposure over many days. Once the infection takes hold, aging ceases, and healing ability is accelerated to such a degree that a wound that would normally heal in a month will fully close up and heal, without a scar, in a matter of minutes. I'm still not sure if we are truly immortal, but if we are not our normal life span extends to thousands of years.

Oh, we can be killed, surely, but not easily. Most injuries will heal. Cut off our heads, or burn our bodies to ashes—that will do the job. Shooting us will not, nor will the traditional stake. Only an injury that makes healing impossible will kill us.

Now it developed that my becoming a vampire was not the only price Meskhenet had in mind. Somehow, perhaps from seeing me around the camp, she had fallen in love with me. It seemed that her usual healing practice did not involve conversion of the patient. This she had reserved for me.

And do not let anyone suggest that a vampire cannot make love in the same manner as any other man. We are not dead, and we are not un-dead—whatever that means—we are as alive as any other, perhaps more so. We can see our reflection in a mirror, and the sun does *less* harm to us than to ordinary people, for with our exaggerated healing abilities even the worst sunburn is no more than a momentary discomfort.

By the time my leg wound had fully healed, and I had been fully converted into a vampire, Meskhenet was no longer visiting my tent once a day. She had moved into my tent and was sharing my bed.

Well, she was beautiful, very smart, a good companion, and a wonderful lover. I think I got the best of the bargain.

But I have not seen her for many years. I feel that she is still alive, though I could not prove it. There was a strong connection born of my conversion, and perhaps a stronger one developed of a marriage—this seems the most appropriate term, even if the union was not blessed by a priest—lasting some 273 years. That's a very long time, and you get to know each other very well. Unfortunately, even perfection eventually pales, and we have long since gone our separate ways, finding others with whom to share a few years. Never again so long, at least for me, for all but one of my partners since Meskhenet have been mortal.

During nearly all of the last two millennia I have followed the profession of arms. Meskhenet was quite right in saying that any blood will nourish, but human blood really does taste best. Battlefields are a reliable source of fresh blood. The donors no longer have any use for it, and the dangers of "dead" blood are nothing more than a literary device. It matters not at all whether the donor is living or dead.

During nearly all of those centuries life has been relatively easy. Because I do not actually have to spend the daylight hours hiding in a coffin—I sleep in a bed, like anyone else, and usually at night—I was in little danger from vampire hunters. On occasion, I even joined in the hunt.

* * *

It was in 1784, in the Austrian province of Styria, where I was then doing service as a captain of infantry. The little village where I was stationed was experiencing an epidemic of vampirism, or so everyone believed. It was *not* me. I was dining regularly, to be sure, but no one was dying of it. As for the epidemic, I believe it was tuberculosis.

But a vampire was suspected, so find it we must. The *Bürgermeister*, a fat little man dressed in rust-colored broadcloth and sagging woolen stockings, organized a group of men with the intention of doing just that. I was present, with two of my men, ostensibly to provide additional protection for the vampire hunters. From my own point of view, I simply joined them for the entertainment value. I never thought that desecrating a corpse was a good thing, but I recognized that it didn't actually hurt the corpse and, in these cases, while "killing" the so-called "vampire"would do nothing to stop the tubercular infection in the village, it would probably make the townspeople feel better.

"Do you suspect anyone in this?" I asked the *Bürgermeister*.

"There have been six who died in the past year," he replied. "It is almost certainly one of them. So we will begin by examining the graves."

Our little party entered the cemetery, going from one new grave to the next, starting with the oldest. The priest, who was supposed to be an expert on vampires, would get down on his hands and knees and closely examine the ground. He had known me for months, so I had to wonder just how perceptive he really was. Today's movies and television shows are quite wrong; we don't have retractable fangs, and we don't change appearance when we're hungry. My canine teeth are significantly longer and sharper than normal, something the priest had apparently never noticed, I suppose because he mostly saw me in his church and it was well known that no vampire could tolerate the presence of the holy, much less take the Eucharist.

"What are you looking for, Father?" I asked.

"Over a vampire's grave," the priest replied, "you will often find several small, deep holes in the ground, about the size of a thumb. He has to get in and out of his grave, you see, and it seems that he can somehow flow up through these holes." He frowned. "But you do not always find them, and if that is the case we shall have to resort to other means."

The priest went back to examining the graves for holes, while my men and I watched. I found it mildly amusing that this priest—in that age a learned man—thought that vampires could somehow turn into liquid or mist and flow up from their graves through holes in the ground. I suppose this was no stranger than the later notion that a 200 pound vampire could somehow transform himself into a two pound bat and then back again. Physics, I suppose, did not constitute a major portion of a theologian's education in those days, and would later simply be ignored by writers of fantastic fiction.

It took perhaps an hour for the priest to concede that none of the suspect graves had the tell-tale holes, so now it was decided that other measures would have to be taken. A thirteen-year-old village boy was brought to the cemetery. Under questioning, the boy attested that he was still a virgin, and had never so much as contemplated indulging in self-abuse, knowing full well the horrible consequences that would certainly ensue. People really believed that back in those days, and were convinced—despite a total lack of any evidence—that such things would lead to physical weakness, insanity, and blindness. Despite which, naturally, everyone did it anyway and simply presumed that *they* were somehow immune from the consequences, but that it was still dangerous for anyone else.

The boy, having no doubt lied about his solitary habits, but probably having been truthful about his virginity, was then mounted on a white stallion. The horse had not yet been put to stud, so here we had a virgin mounted upon another virgin.

Taking the horse by the reins, a man then led it through the cemetery, being careful to lead it across each of the suspect graves in turn. The horse plodded along placidly, to the thorough frustration of the vampire hunters, who expected it to balk at the vampire's grave, the double virginity of the horse and boy—purity mounted upon purity, as it were—was supposed to naturally shy from the evil contained in the grave.

This new device having failed, the *Bürgermeister* announced that they would have to resort to the hard way and dig up each suspect. Shovels were procured and the men set to work, my troops included. Being their leader, I naturally employed my time in sitting on a bench under a tree chatting with the *Bürgermeister*, who, also being a leader, was no more inclined to indulge in physical labor than I.

The oldest graves yielded nothing more than a horrible stench and rotting corpses. They found the vampire in the newest, buried little more than two months. The occupant, in life a rather attractive young lady, was now bloated, with blood seeping from her nose and mouth. More blood stained her white garment. There was, really, nothing at all unusual about her corpse, which was simply decomposing, but the priest assured us that these signs clearly pointed to the girl being a vampire.

Under the priest's direction, a wooden stake was driven through the girl's heart, in response to which she emitted a pitiable groan. I am sure this was nothing more than some remaining air or gases being driven up through her throat by the pressure, but it certainly convinced the vampire hunters that they had found the right body. One of the men then cut off her head with a sexton's shovel and placed it in the bottom of the coffin, between her feet. After that they cut off enough of the stake to allow the coffin to be closed and refilled the grave.

"Now we shall be safe," the priest informed us. "We have released that poor girl from her curse, and perhaps her soul will now return to God, if she has not already been irredeemably damned for her depredations. We can hope, at least."

I doubted that the girl had ever done anything deserving of eternal punishment. Certainly she wasn't a vampire. Quite possibly, she had been in heaven ever since she died, or, equally, when you're dead you're dead and that's all there is. I really have no particular knowledge of what follows life, nor do I expect to gain any such knowledge until my own is over.

In any event, the putative vampire having been vanquished, life returned to normal in the little village. The epidemic ended, not, I am sure, because of the townspeople having mutilated the poor girl's corpse, but because epidemics generally *do* end after a time.

*   *   *

The biggest problem in my life is that I do not age. I have now been physically in my early 20s for over 2,000 years. The result was that I could never put down permanent roots in any one place. Eventually the neighbors notice that sort of thing. I had to move about every ten years or so. If I liked a place, I might stretch it to 15 years, but never more than that. And after perhaps 30 years had passed I could return, for then, even if those same neighbors *did* recognize me, the fact that they were now closing in on 60 and I appeared to be about 23 would make my declaration that I was their old neighbor's son seem perfectly logical.

This is becoming more difficult now. Today there is DNA. Today fingerprints are not only a positive identifier, but reside in a computerized database that may yet unintentionally discover that I am not only walking around today, but was also an Armor officer in World War II. Today there are entire government agencies devoted to making sure that everyone is who he claims to be. They are looking for terrorists, which I certainly am not, but I know I would make them more than a little curious if they once noticed me. People are supposed to be born, live for seventy or eighty years, and then drop dead. They're not supposed to just keep on living. That sort of thing makes people nervous. There have been too many stories, movies, television shows, and mostly about predatory vampires. The idea that there might be utterly *innocuous* vampires doesn't fit the belief system.

I know where I came from, but I can hardly put Herculaneum on an American government form. And it is no longer possible to lay claim to the identity of some poor child who died within days of birth. Today the government matches birth and death certificates to prevent exactly that sort of thing. Today you need to find a way to create an identity from scratch, which is much harder, but can be done if you know enough about computers.

For now, I am known as Sidney Height, and should I put in a request, Pennsylvania's electronic records would spit out a certified birth certificate indicating that I was born in Pittsburgh in 1984. You always pick a large city for this sort of thing. People know each other in small towns. In a large city you can be anonymous. People don't find it at all odd even if several people they know to be from the same city don't know each other. As often as not today, even people who were in the same high school graduating class may never have met.

I rather count on that sort of thing.

One advantage of being a couple thousand years old is that you have plenty of time to accumulate wealth. If you don't have to work you can remain more anonymous. I have a number of bank accounts, scattered across the country, as well as in the usual havens, Switzerland, the Cayman

Islands, and so forth. But most of my wealth is in tangible assets, real estate, gold, and particularly diamonds. I also hold a lot of stock, much of it purchased in 1929 when the shares were as cheap as they would ever be, and periodically "inherited" from a previous self.

I try to keep a low profile. It is better not to be noticed, though this doesn't always work.

My current home is isolated, a large brick mansard Victorian set in the middle of a wooded 35 acre plot. It looks a bit like something from Charles Addams, though much better maintained. You reach it by driving back almost half a mile into the woods on a brick-paved driveway, shaded in the summer by big oak trees planted along the drive. In the winter, with the leaves gone, the drive looks a bit more ominous.

I have lived here for twelve years now. The forested setting provides most of my needs. The woods are full of animals, giving me a handy blood supply. I am, and always have been, a fairly skilled hunter.

But it appears I may soon need to move again.

It happened on Saturday. I was in the garage, washing one of my cars, when I heard a vehicle coming up the drive. I wasn't expecting anyone.

The vehicle was soon in view, a beat-up Chevy van, once royal blue, but now faded to some indeterminate color in the bluish family. It stopped in front of the house and five people got out, three girls and two boys, all of them appearing to be about eighteen or nineteen except for one of the girls, who appeared to be in her late twenties.

As they were all carrying pistols, the older girl in her right hand, the others stuck into their belts, I quickly decided that this was not a friendly visit.

They walked quite boldly up to the front door. By this time I had slipped around behind the bushes to where I could observe them. The older girl rang the bell several times. As I had moved around to the front of the house and was watching them from behind a hedge, no one answered. I would not have done so in any case. While not readily visible unless you're looking very carefully, there are cameras covering the doors. The presence of armed people on my porch would have suggested that answering the bell wasn't very prudent.

"No one home," the older girl, who appeared to be the leader, informed her companions, slipping her gun into the waistband of her jeans.

She nodded to one of the boys, flipping her right thumb in the direction of the van. The boy trotted to the vehicle and returned with a crowbar, which he applied to the locked door. I have good locks, but my house isn't exactly a bank vault. He had the door open in a few seconds and the five of them went inside.

It was time, I thought, to interrupt their party. Staying behind the hedge and plantings, I moved around to the side of the house and entered by way of the bulkhead door to the basement. I could hear people walking around upstairs.

The house was built in 1887, by a true eccentric. It was right up to date for the time, and subsequent owners, myself included, have spent a lot of money keeping it that way, at least as far as heat, air conditioning, electricity, and so forth are concerned. The story was that the original builder had been a fan of Gothic fiction and had built the house accordingly—complete with a number of hidden passages inside the walls. These passages were not documented anywhere, so far as I could tell, but I had managed to find all of them in the time I'd lived in the house.

Slipping through a concealed door at the back of what had once been a coal cellar, I passed along a short hall built into the base of a fireplace and climbed a wooden ladder to the main floor. I found myself in a small, windowless room. Another ladder led up to the second floor, and a narrow passage continued toward the rear of the house. A low, square door would allow access into the formal parlor at the front of the house. From the other side the door was invisible, the edges concealed in the vertical beading of the mahogany wainscoting.

I could hear the intruders in the parlor. Near the concealed door, a hot-air register looked into the room. Behind the ornamental brass grillwork a small periscope allowed me to see into the parlor. The leader was seated on the window seat, dispatching the others to the rest of the house to discover what looked good. They had already piled some of my property on the coffee table. I saw none of the true treasures. They had taken some nice watches from my bedroom, and had accumulated a fair stock of jewelry. Yet no one had bothered to take down the small painting that hung on the wall within a few feet of their booty. I have owned that painting for many years, having purchased it from the artist, so it was "unknown" to the art world in general, but I suspect it would bring more than the house and the entire 35-acre estate should I ever decide to sell it. There are no doubt very, very few undiscovered Da Vincis in the world, but this was one of them.

I decided it would be best to start with the boys, who were physically bigger and stronger than the girls. When the leader sent one of them to check out the attic I decided that was a good place to start.

Knowing the hidden passages and stairs far better than the intruders knew the ordinary ones, I was in the attic before the young man arrived. There was plenty for him to look through up there. Not only did it contain things that I had stored, but there were chests, cabinets, and trunks long abandoned by former owners. He was bending over an open steamer trunk, rummaging through the contents, when I slipped up behind him and hit him over the head with an old Indian club.

There was a very satisfying crunch as the heavy club fractured his skull, and he went down instantly, without making a sound beyond the thump of his body across the trunk. I briefly pondered taking the opportunity of a snack, but decided there were more pressing matters to consider. There were still four people in my house who didn't belong there and I wanted them out.

I slipped back into the hidden staircase and went to find the next intruder. I really wanted to take out the two men first. Call it chivalry or something, killing the men first. None of these people were going to leave the house alive.

I found the other boy in the library. Unfortunately, he caught sight of me in a mirror as I was slipping up on him. Before I could get to him he had his gun out and put a bullet into my side. It didn't hit anything vital—it couldn't, really, and the wound would heal completely in a few minutes—but it made noise, which was something I had been trying to avoid.

He didn't get a chance to take a second shot. One thing the fiction writers got right was the astonishing speed and strength we can muster when needed. Before he could pull the trigger again I was across the room, had torn the gun from his hand, and lifted him right off the floor.

"You picked the wrong house," I said, opening my mouth as wide as I could manage and hissing in my best Christopher Lee imitation.

The effect seemed to work. The kid shrieked and wet his pants as I pulled him down and ripped out his throat with my teeth. I really don't do that sort of thing very often—it's messy, if you must know—but it just seemed appropriate now.

I didn't take the time to do more than sip quickly. Between the noise of the gun and the kid's screaming I figured his friends would be in there before long. I opened the bookcase door and disappeared back into the wall.

A minute later all three girls were in the library, guns in their hands, standing over their dead accomplice.

"What the hell is this?" the blond one demanded.

The older one, already established as the leader, got down on one knee and examined the dead burglar. The look on her face was one of bewilderment, mixed with curiosity. Obviously she had been expecting to pull off a burglary, not to suddenly find herself in the middle of a horror movie. Still, it seemed somehow to affect her less than it did the other two. As if there was something natural about it.

"Something tore his throat out," she said.

That would be me, I thought.

"What would do that?"

"Damned if I know." Her voice sounded odd, as if she thought that perhaps she *did* know, but wasn't quite ready to admit it to herself. She looked around. "Where's Billy?"

Billy, I presumed, was the corpse in the attic. He would not be joining them.

Having decided to keep the mess confined to one room, I slipped out into the hall through another door hidden in the wainscoting and quickly closed and locked the library door. Now I had them trapped, and it was just a matter of figuring out how to dispatch them.

The problem was simply that there were three of them, each armed, and I didn't want to be shot again. Even if they couldn't kill me, being shot was still painful and I preferred to avoid it.

I could kill the electricity in that room. Darkness would be to my advantage, except it was only a little after one in the afternoon and the windows would let in plenty of light. There were shutters, but they were merely ornamental, bolted to the outside walls alongside the windows.

I wondered if it was time to resort to costuming. Even with a vampire's fangs, I suspected I didn't present a particularly terrifying image. At the moment I was dressed as I had been while washing the car, old blue jeans, sneakers, and a white tee-shirt. The tee-shirt was rather gory, both from the kid's blood, and from a little of my own, where I had bled until the bullet wound healed up. I supposed that might help, though the full outfit of black suit and opera cape might be more effective.

Except, again, it was the middle of the day. People these days are conditioned by movies and television to think that vampires can only be out at night. By popular image, I should have been safely tucked away in a coffin in some hidden crypt in the sub-basement. If I turned up in the library dressed like Dracula the first reaction was more likely to be amusement than terror, even with their dead companion to remind them of what they were facing.

Nevertheless, I ran down to the basement and pulled the fuses for the library. Even if there was still light from the windows, it would be darker than before and that had to help.

Leaving the three girls to ponder this new development, I quickly ran up to my room and changed shirts, getting rid of the bloody tee-shirt and slipping into a black turtleneck.

Before returning to my vantage point inside the library wall I went outside and disabled their van by pulling the wires off the spark plugs. It could be repaired in less than a minute, but you would have to know what was wrong first, and I am still male enough to think that it might take a woman a while to figure out that the neatly replaced plug hole covers concealed disconnected terminals. Perhaps this is overly technical, stereotypical thinking, but I'm 2,081 years old, so indulge me if I sometimes seem old fashioned. I've spent a lot more of my life in the "old days" than in the modern ones.

The precaution was well advised. I had barely finished and closed the hood when the three girls came around the corner of the house. I presumed from this that they had opened one of the library windows and lowered themselves to the ground outside the house. It was a drop of about ten feet; not too far, really, presuming you were careful.

I ducked behind a hedge and waited to see what they would do.

All three had their guns out as they piled into the van. As the starter ground away I could see determination turning to dismay. It took a few seconds, but as they realized what was happening—or, more precisely, what was *not* happening—the fear was obvious on their faces.

I heard the clunk of the hood release and one of them got out of the van, coming around to the front of the vehicle and raising the hood. She was peering at the engine as the leader turned it over. I didn't think she'd see anything, and the sound of the engine turning over should have been enough to drown out the sharp pop of the sparks jumping to the sides of the metal wells. Unless she pulled on one of the wires she was unlikely to notice anything.

My vantage point was only about eight feet from the front of the van, on the passenger side. With the windowless side door closed—the girl checking the engine had been in the front seat—I would be mostly shielded from the view of anyone in the van.

I took the chance. I move extremely fast, so almost before the leader sitting in the driver's seat could realize that her comrade had suddenly vanished I had dragged the girl back behind the hedge and snapped her neck. I almost felt sorry for her, as she didn't die immediately. The look in her eye was one of curiosity more than pain; consciousness was rapidly fading, for her spinal cord was severed and she couldn't breathe.

Fascinating as this might from an academic viewpoint, there was no time to waste. I picked up her gun, a pre-war Belgian Browning Hi-Power, with the rudimentary fixed sights and flat wooden grips, and looked around the hedge. The other two girls were out of the van now. It seemed to me that it was time for direct action.

"Perhaps," I said, stepping from behind the hedge, my gun pointed between them, "you should consider surrendering."

It was a rather ingenuous suggestion, really. I was going to kill both of them whether they gave up or not. I just thought that it would be easier all around if no one else shot me today. The fact that this cannot really harm me is secondary to the fact that it still hurts like hell.

"Maybe *you* should give up," the leader said. "There are two of us and only one of you."

I smiled. "Half an hour ago there were *five* of you and only one of me. I still like the odds."

The younger girl swung her gun toward me and pulled the trigger. Her bullet zipped past my waist, clipping a belt loop but not touching anything else. *So be it,* I thought.

I fired back, automatically squeezing the trigger twice. Both 9 mm slugs slammed into the girl's chest. She would have been dead before she started to fall.

The leader took advantage of the situation and fired a carefully aimed shot into my lower abdomen. Normally, such a shot would have been instantly disabling, even if it didn't kill. Normally. Of course, I'm not normal.'

"Damn!" I grunted. "That hurt!"

Then I shot the remaining girl right through the heart.

Instead of falling down, she shot me again. Twice. Then I shot *her* again, with equally inconsequential results.

"Well, hell," I said. "Do you really want to keep doing this? It seems so pointless."

The girl had lowered her gun and was leaning against the front of the van. "I suppose not," she said.

"Why were you robbing my house? With them?"

"It seemed like a good idea at the time." She was poking at the hole in her shirt where the bullet had gone in. "This is nearly healed," she said, sounding surprised.

"Naturally. Did you expect otherwise?"

She glanced at her dead companion. "I'm a little new at this," she said.

I looked down at the dead girl, thinking about the three other bodies in and around my house. There obviously would not be a fifth, which made it important to get to know this girl a little better. Would I be moving immediately, or did I have some time?

"You should have been taught," I said. "You didn't get this way accidentally. The one who converts you has an obligation to teach you."

"He's dead. We were in a car wreck—it took his head off. He never got the chance."

"Then perhaps you need a new teacher? Does anyone know you're here?"

She shook her head. "Only the rest of my crew, and they're all dead now, I suppose."

"Close friends, were they?"

"No. I put this crew together for this job. I hardly knew them, except that they were supposed to be good and didn't seem to worry about whether they hurt anyone."

"Then I suggest we remove the bodies to someplace a bit more discreet. You might also wish to have something to eat, as it seems to have been rather conveniently supplied. Repairing bullet wounds takes a bit out of you."

*　　*　　*

Her name, it developed, was Laura, and she was a burglar by profession. At least, she had been until about a year ago, when she started to get sick. Over the course of several months she had started to waste away, and when the diagnosis of pancreatic cancer was received she was weak enough already to accept the inevitability of death. There was a less than five percent survival rate, her doctor informed her, mostly because that particular form of cancer was generally painless until it was too late to do anything about it.

She had gone into the hospital, presumably for the last time, when an orderly began to visit her. He made the same offer that Meskhenet had made me. Desperate, she accepted, and two weeks later walked out of the hospital, still thin enough to look a bit unhealthy, but now essentially immortal.

She went to live with the orderly, but he had barely begun to teach her when he was decapitated in a car wreck. Most things a vampire can recover from, but not beheading. Not knowing what else to do, Laura returned to her former profession, recruiting the four younger burglars specifically for the attack on my house. She had no real idea of who I was, but I was known to live alone, on a large estate, and presumably had more than a few things worth stealing.

"If I was going to live forever," she told me, "I figured I should start accumulating stuff. I can't be a burglar forever, after all."

"Nor shall you be in the future," I said. "Stay here a while. You have a great deal to learn, and there aren't that many who can teach you."

Did I mention that she was quite beautiful? She was of about average height, slender, with short, dark-brown hair that was still growing back from the chemotherapy. We heal very rapidly, but some things, such as hair and nails, grow at a normal rate. She would be pleasant to be around for a few years. And I liked the fact that she was of only average height, for while I was considered quite a tall man in Roman times, at 5' 9" I am rather on the short side of average today.

She nodded, looking around the room. We were sitting in the dining room, side by side at the long table, with tall wine glasses in front of us. They did not contain wine. Her accomplices were providing a final service to us.

What will come next? Laura's career as a thief is over, I think. I can show her far less dangerous ways to gain wealth. A vampire would not do well in prison. Too much surveillance tends to interfere with our dietary habits.

Time would tell. And time was one thing we would have in plenty.

THE LIFE OF SALMIK THE GREAT

[This is another of the mid-'70s Gehunite Empire stories. Ostensibly written by Gehunite historian Ran Kulnahur during the pre-industrial period of the Empire, it takes rather a fairy tale style, though it's not a story for children.]

I
His Unusual Birth and Upbringing

In the old days the principal business of the ancient island Kingdom of Kaam was piracy. Kaamites were pirates in the same way that Ferians were bankers, or the women of Callaa soldiers. It was what they did, it was what they were expected to do, and no one really thought that much about it.

Hardly a day passed when a Kaamite vessel didn't depart from the capitol's harbour, intent on the capture of whatever foreign merchantman she happened to encounter. There were Kaamite merchantmen, too, naturally, for the little country carried on a brisk trade with the rest of the world. It was simply that they acquired their stock in trade by stealing it from others. Perhaps this sounds odd to us now, but once upon a time that was how things worked. Pirates weren't villains, they were tradesmen. At least in Kaam.

It was in the great port city of Virkulla, on the northeast coast of Kaam, that Ilkul Darwika, the "admiral" of a fleet of 17 well equipped and well founded pirate ships, made his headquarters.

Darwika was born on the 19th day of Twomonth, in 1742 of the old system, which was 75 BG by our current reckoning. He was an average looking man, with brown hair and grey eyes, standing 185 CM, and blessed with one of those deep, pleasant voices that seem to automatically command obedience. He was a natural leader, and when he was 12 he was entered as Apprentice on his Uncle Argul's only ship.

He learned quickly, so by the time he was aged 20 years, and eligible to sit for his Master's licence, he was more than ready. He had been serving as First Mate for three years by then, and had earned sufficient prize money—much of it as the result of the fortuitous capture of an Arzucaldan treasure ship—to purchase an elderly frigate, which would become the foundation of his own fleet.

When he was 25, Darwika married Tulia Vahndur, the 17 year old daughter of a fellow fleet owner (Darwika had added two more frigates by that time). He was becoming wealthy, and Darwika brought his new bride home to a brand new villa in the suburbs of Virkulla. And it was in this elegantly furnished house, on the 12th day of Threemonth, 1769 (48 BG), that his only daughter was born.

The child, which they named Sulae, after Ilkul's grandmother, grew into a slim, beautiful young woman. By the time she was 16, and had finished her schooling, she was much sought after as a potential wife. Not only was she beautiful, but she was much praised for her intelligence and wit. A perfect bride for some wealthy young ship owner or captain, everyone said.

Sulae was tall, 175 CM, yet weighed only 45 KG. Her hair was long, lustrous, and black as a starless night, and her eyes were a soft grey, very like her father's. When she spoke her voice was warm and gentle, and her figure, displayed by the clinging, translucent gowns favoured by wealthy Kaamite women, was as near perfect as one might encounter outside an art museum.

But it was during her 16th year that everything changed for the girl. There was a meadow behind her father's house, bordering a dense forest, and it had been Sulae's habit to wander through that meadow in the warmth of the afternoon, gathering flowers. At times she wandered into the fringes of the forest, where the thick briar patches furnished succulent berries. She had no fear of the place. Kaam had been settled for centuries, and all of the dangerous animals had long since been killed.

One warm afternoon, as she was walking near the edge of the forest, the branches suddenly parted and a great, grey wolf stepped boldly from the trees and stood directly in her path. Sulae gave a start, for the animal was huge, and she wondered where it had come from. There were no wild wolves on Kaam, she was sure of that. Had is escaped from the zoological garden? Was it someone's pet?

She wasn't afraid. She knew that, even in the wild, healthy, well-fed wolves preferred not to attack people, or even to stay around them. Yet this wolf was different. He seemed somehow more formidable than any wolf she had ever seen, larger, even, than 'old Tosh,' the star attraction at the

Virkulla Zoo, who the keepers had long claimed to be the biggest wolf in the world.

The wolf began to move toward her, and Sulae began cautiously backing away. She still wasn't really afraid. There was something about the great beast that seemed to banish fear. Still, she was moving back toward the house, where there would be people and, if need be, weapons. But as she did so, she tripped over a tuft of grass, falling full length on her back on the soft turf.

The wolf was standing over her at once, his forepaws pinning her shoulders to the ground. Somehow she knew what was happening, and at the same time she didn't quite believe it. She was quite sure you didn't do that sort of thing with an animal. She had never even done that sort of thing with a human.

When it was over, the wolf trotted back to the edge of the forest, looking back over his shoulder at her. She was sure he winked before vanishing among the trees.

For a time, Sulae lay on the grass, unable to move, wondering why the animal had behaved in such an unusual way. And then her father was picking her up, and carrying her back to the house, where a maid carefully bathed her and put her to bed.

Two months later the doctor confirmed that she was pregnant. This was impossible, Sulae was sure, but the doctor insisted that she was. When she refused to say who was responsible, he simply put that down to an unusual modesty. Kaamites didn't prize virginity, the way Arzucaldans did, but Kaamites worshipped L'Mik, who was in general one of the more sensible gods, while Arzucaldan's worshipped dozens of gods, all of whom agreed that virginity was *very* important, and that women belonged to the fathers when they were young, and needed to be conveyed to their husbands intact.

Kaamite women generally thought that Arzucaldan men were idiots, but the fact remained that the only women in Arzucalda who didn't quite literally "belong" to a man were Callaaite mercenaries. It would take an idiot, or a lunatic, to try to tame one of those.

From Sulae's point of view, the obvious problem with the doctor's diagnosis was that she couldn't be pregnant because, unusual as the wolf's behaviour had been, wolves couldn't make humans pregnant. Her father knew, certainly, but being a sensible fellow, he told her that, should anyone ask, the father was a young seaman on shore leave, and who had returned to his ship and been killed.

"Whatever happens," Darwika told her, "we cannot allow the truth to be known. If it is, the king might find out."

The girl was puzzled. "What if he does?" she asked. "Why should he care, other than that it is certainly a curiosity."

"Because," he father said, "I am fairly sure that wolf was *not* a normal wolf at all."

"Obviously. No normal wolf would have done that. I suppose," she said, being practical, "that he escaped from a bordello. He was probably trained to do that, to perform in a show."

"Or perhaps he wasn't a wolf at all."

"Of course he was."

"Then how are you pregnant, daughter? No wolf could do that to you, and that certainly wasn't a man wearing a wolf hide. So close, you would certainly have noticed, wouldn't you?"

"I suppose."

Darwika went to a shelf and took down a slim volume, the black leather cover worn soft and supple from years of reading, the pages well thumbed. "It's in here," he said.

"*The Book of L'Mik?* What do you mean, father?"

Kaamites, as I have said, worshipped L'Mik even then. The Book was found in every house.

Darwika opened the book and flipped through the pages until he found the passage he was looking for.

"And know," he read, " that in the days to come,
A virgin girl shall in a meadow here
Be mated with a wolf, and that wolf me,
And from that union there shall come a child
Unlike to any child that ever liv'd,
For he shall be the one son of L'Mik,
And grow to be a king more powerful
Than any who did ever come before.
And on him I shall found an empire then,
That he and his descendants shall enlarge,
To be the greatest that the earth shall know."

The girl shook her head. "I don't know," she said. "I'm sure the description fits, but why would he choose me? I'm not even particularly religious. I've read through the book, naturally, but not all that carefully. I can't say I even remembered that part."

"Who knows how a god thinks?" her father said. "It sounds plausible to me, which is the important thing. The important thing is that since it *was* a wolf that made you pregnant, it would be very unwise to allow the word to reach the king. King Fornik is sure to know of this prophecy, or, if he doesn't, one of his advisors certainly does. The king is nervous enough as it is, so he'll certainly make sure the prophecy isn't fulfilled unless it's his own daughter who fulfills it. And the princess is *not* a virgin."

So the secret was kept, and on the 25th day of Threemonth, 1786 (31 BG), a fine, healthy baby boy came into the world. His mother named him Salmik, after her Uncle Sa, her mother's elder brother, and the god her own father was convinced had sired him. He was a very large baby, 7.7 KG at birth, yet he came into the world in the usual way with, if anything, rather *less* discomfort than was usual with a much smaller infant.

By the time the boy was 13, and had finished his formal schooling, Salmik was something of a marvel. Exactly how he came to be conceived remained a secret, but his accomplishment did not. Nor did his unusual size. At 13 he had already reached a height of 183 CM, and weighed 88 KG, with a hard, muscled body that promised great power at full growth.

Like his mother's, his hair was jet black, and he had inherited the family's grey eyes. His quick grasp of every subject had astonished his teachers, and he was fluent not only in the languages of Kaam and Gehun, which are, after all, closely related, but also in Arzucaldan, Callaaish, Dushite, Karhafaran, Ibosian, Iorian, and Ferian. There were very few people in the world he couldn't converse with. Nor was his knowledge of mathematics anything short of astonishing.

His schooling finished, Salmik was entered as Apprentice in one of his grandfather's frigates, quickly proving that his natural genius included seamanship. Within a year he had advanced, entirely on merit, to First Mate, and there he stayed until he was 20, the earliest age at which Kaamite law allowed a man to be licenced as Master.

By then he had reached his full height of 200 CM, and weighed a muscular 120 KG. He had grown a full beard and moustache, both as black as his hair, and was deeply tanned from years at sea.

His first command was the brand new frigate *Raven*, which his grandfather had specially built for his grandson. The cabin overhead was high enough for him to stand erect without having to duck under deck beams, a luxury no other ship would afford for a man of his stature.

The first cruise of *Raven* was marked by an indecisive battle with a Callaaite merchantman, which proved to be a troop transport. There was simply no way such a battle could end well for the Kaamites, and after sufficient *pro forma* sparring to satisfy honour, the ships parted.

An hour later, they met again, exchanged signals as if nothing had happened, and Salmik invited the Callaaite captain aboard to dine with him. He was a wise man, even at so young an age, and no doubt understood that it would serve him well to stay on friendly terms with these astonishing northern warrior women.

A few days later, *Raven* was seriously damaged in a storm, with her mizzen carried away. This was replaced at sea, and a story was thereafter told that Salmik had single-handedly lifted the new mast into place. This was told as a way of confirming his crew's opinion that their captain was somehow rather more than human.

Other damage, however, required docking, so *Raven* put in at the Gehunite port of Fullah to make repairs.

II
His Surprising Marriage

Mira Torgenhuli was far from young. She was, if you please, a plump, perhaps even fat, white-haired woman who had seen the earth circle the sun 81 times. She lived alone in a wretched house not far from the Fullah dockyard. Her husband, Ardorik, had been dead for 33 years, and her only income was the tiny widow's pension a miserly government allowed her. She received that only because he had been a warrant officer in the Royal Gehunite Navy, and had been killed in a sea battle.

The pension was enough to pay the rent on her hovel, and to buy enough food to keep her alive, but nothing more. True, some would say that she must have been finding enough to eat, given her tiny frame and great weight. Mira was sure she was fat simply because she was fat, and not because she ate too much. She never felt that she ever managed to eat enough.

Perhaps, had there been children, they might have helped her, given her a nicer home, better food. Food that would satisfy her hunger without making her fat. But she had no children, and now she spent her declining years in solitude, finding her only solace in the promise of a better life in heaven offered by her faith to anyone who lived a good life.

As poor as she was, she did not turn away an elderly beggar, who came to her door asking for a few scraps. Instead, she invited the old man in, gave him to eat, and provided him a place to sleep by the miserable fire. No doubt it was warmer than the street.

The next morning, she awoke to find the man gone, and in his place was a giant grey wolf, lazing comfortably before a roaring fire. Curiously, her first reaction was to wonder where the wood had come from. Even if he'd emptied the wood box, there hadn't been enough for such a blaze.

As for the animal, it sat up when she came into the room and nodded amiably.

Oddly, she found she wasn't at all afraid of it. She sat on a chair near the fire, and the animal laid its head upon her lap, looking very content as she petted its massive head. "Now," she said, "just where did you come from? You didn't eat the old man, did you?"

The wolf looked at her curiously, and a deep, resonant voice that seemed to bypass her ears and communicate directly with her brain replied, "I *was* the old man."

"You're not talking, but I can hear you."

"Wolves cannot talk. But you can hear my thoughts."

"How very curious. But you seem a nice enough wolf."

The animal nodded. "You were kind to me when I was the old man, Mira Torgenhuli. You shall be rewarded for this."

"This is all very strange." She found that she was not speaking aloud, and that apparently the wolf could hear her thoughts just as clearly as she could hear his.

"What is the one thing in life you desired most, but never had?"

"Children. My husband could not give me children. But he was perfect in every other way."

"Then you shall have children."

"At 81? It's much too late for me."

"With me," the wolf said in her mind, "the calendar is meaningless. Time is as nothing to me, nor will it be to you. Look at your hand."

She looked down at the hand stroking the wolf's head and gasped. The hand, and the arm where it emerged from her sleeve, was slender and unwrinkled, the skin smooth and unmarked.

Looking up, she caught sight of herself in the mirror. The face that looked back was unlined, beautiful, framed by a thick cascade of chestnut coloured hair. It was a face she hadn't seen in many years, since before her marriage to Ardorik.

Her dress hung on her like a shapeless sack. The fat was gone, her body that of a young woman again.

"What is this? How did you?"

The wolf lifted its head from her lap and sat by the fire. "You will find a new dress laid out on your bed," he told her. "You will find that it fits perfectly, and is in the latest style. Bathe yourself and put it on. You will also find gold clips for your hair, and a gold chain for your neck. When you have washed and dressed, go to the dockyard and find a Kaamite frigate called *Raven*. Ask to see her captain, and tell him that his father sent you to be with him."

Mira nodded, afraid that saying anything, even thinking anything, might bring an early wakening from this odd dream. For by now, she was convinced that she *was* dreaming.

So she went into her bedroom, and there, on her bed, was a beautiful new dress, together with the gold hair clips and necklace. It was all she could do to fill the tub and bathe, so much did she want to put on the dress before she awakened.

Yet she couldn't help lingering in the bath, marvelling at the perfect body she now had. More perfect, she thought, than it had been when she was 17, which was about the age she thought this body to be. Still, the face was certainly hers, or had been when she was younger. Mira had been quite a beautiful young woman, before she became old and fat.

At last, she dressed herself. As the wolf had told her, the dress fit perfectly. It was made of deep blue silk, and left most of her back bare. One perfect leg flashed through a long slit in the right side of the skirt as she walked. There were also boots waiting for her by the bed, made of brilliantly shined black leather that fit tightly around her calves, and somehow these boots, though they looked brand new, seemed to be fully broken in and quite comfortable.

She found that she was having a little trouble adjusting to this new reality. By now she knew she wasn't dreaming. She was young and beautiful again, but if she now again had the body of a 17-year-old girl, she still had the mind and experience of an 81-year-old woman.

She ventured out about mid-day, finding the frigate after about an hour of searching. There was some trouble with the guard at the brow, who obviously thought it would be better to keep this beautiful young woman for himself, rather than pass her on to the captain.

Mira was rather delighted. She hadn't caused that sort of reaction in a man in a very long time. Until that morning, the guard would no doubt have been more than happy to get rid of her.

After a few minutes, a young officer appeared and she was allowed aboard. "Are you the captain?" she asked.

"I'm afraid not," he replied. "I am called Sandav Romiwero, second mate. Are you sure it's the captain you want to see?"

"I was told to see him. Yes."

"Who told you?"

"I was sent by…" She stopped. How could she possibly explain who sent her? "He said, tell the captain that his father sent me."

Romiwero blinked. The captain's father had died at sea many years ago, before he was born. That was common knowledge. Or had he merely run away, and now was sending this young woman to make the first overtures toward a reconciliation? "Wait here," he said. "I'll see if the captain is busy."

When Salmik came on deck, it was Mira's turn to be astonished. Never in her life had she seen such a huge man. "Come with me," he said, leading her under the quarterdeck to his cabin.

"Now," Salmik said, when they were alone, "you say my *father* sent you?"

"That's what he told me to say."

"What did he look like?"

"At first, he looked like an old man. Quite old. Nearly as old as me."

"Then he can't have been that old, can he?"

Mira decided this was going to take some getting used to. She knew how old she was, but no one looking at now would ever believe it. "I'm older than I look."

"How old? Perhaps 20 at the most."

"My birthday was last month. I was 81."

Salmik sat on the edge of his desk and looked at her. "Fascinating," he replied.

"It's true."

"You said," the captain went on, "that *at first* he seemed like an old man. What do you mean?"

"Yes. Last night he was an old man, a beggar, looking for food and a place to rest for the night. I found him some scraps, and let him sleep by my fire. But when I awoke this morning, the old man was gone, and in his place was a huge, grey wolf."

"A wolf?"

"A very nice wolf, really. And he could talk. Or he could make you hear his words without talking, I suppose. He said that, as a reward for my kindness to the old man I should be young again. And I am."

Salmik nodded gravely. "And the wolf said he was my father?"

"Yes. It was very odd."

The captain remembered the stories his mother and grandfather had told him, when they believed him old enough not to repeat them. Odd indeed.

A week later, when *Raven* departed Fullah, Mira remained aboard as Salmik's bride. She stayed by his side as the ship cruised here and there, taking prizes and building his fortune. But she did not become pregnant, as she had expected. Neither, oddly, did she seem to age. It was as if she was to remain 17 forever.

Salmik's grandfather died in late 1817 (2 BG), a distinguished old gentleman pirate, leaving his grandson as sole owner of the family fleet, which by now numbered 34 ships. But it was Mira who suggested there might be a better use for them than piracy.

"The people of Gehun are tired of the government there," she said. "A handful of rich people control everything, including the king, and the people have nothing. You're destined to rule, my husband. You know that. An empire is yours to found. L'Mik said as much centuries ago. Why not found it in Gehun?"

"How should I do that?" Salmik asked. "I have a fleet, but my men are sailors, not soldiers. And we would obviously need soldiers to take on Gehun's army."

"Then hire them. Take your ships and sail to Callaa. You're rich enough, you can easily hire an army there. They might not even have to fight. The Gehunite army loves the king and the wealthy no more than the common people. Put a Callaaite army in front of them and they may just decide that changing sides is the best course."

Her husband nodded. There was much wisdom in that. Alone in the world, Callaa had learnt the secret of making steel. Their swords and armour were much lighter, and much stronger, than the iron weapons everyone else was forced to use. Their soldiers might all be women—it was illegal for men to bear arms in Callaa, though the men were the ones who made the steel and forged the weapons from it—but they had a reputation as the most dangerous fighters in the world. Even without weapons. Blond she-demons from the iron bound north, many called them.

And so Salmik sailed to Callaa, and negotiated with the queen in the airy palace at Callaahavn. In exchange for a great deal of money, a quarter of it going into the royal treasury and the rest paid to the soldiers, he filled his ships with Callaaite mercenaries and boldly sailed for Tufaria Bay, on the Ghehunite coast, the home of the main Gehunite naval anchorage at Koril Harbour, with the capital city spread out above the bay.

The campaign lasted six weeks. As Mira had predicted, very often the mere sight of the Callaaite mercenaries in their gleaming armour was enough to convince the Gehunite troops where wisdom lay.

Six weeks after he had defeated the Gehunite Royal Navy, or what little of it had been in harbour, Salmik Darwika entered the royal palace in Tufaria and his wife placed the crown on his head. Appropriately, it was the New Year's Holiday, and on that day Salmik declared that a new age had begun.

"This will now be the Age of Gehun," he told the gathered nobles and people. "On this New Year's Holiday we begin a new calendar. The first year of the Empire of Gehun."

There were smiles at that. Gehun was a kingdom, not an empire. Not ever a very powerful kingdom, despite having the same name as the continent. Merely a small, peninsular country. Not that important.

Salmik noticed the smiles, but he could see things these men could not. "From this beginning," he went on, "we shall carve out an empire such as the world has never seen before. An empire that will circle the globe. An empire, indeed, that in the years to come will *be* the world, where all of humanity will unite under one flag, where all will have justice, where everyone will find equal access to my ear."

III
His Empire Expands

Just as he had promised, Salmik began at once to expand his new empire. Gehun itself was, at that time, quite a small nation. Just a narrow peninsula on the southeastern corner of the continent. But within a very few years its power was being felt over the rest of the continent. Gehun's armies were constantly on the march, always adding new territory to the Empire.

An Imperial Constitution, said to be mostly the work of the Empress, was draughted and adopted on the 17th day of Twomonth, in the third year of the Empire, and it was this single document, more than the power of Gehun's armies, that led to the successful expansion of the Empire.

When a nation was conquered, they found the occupiers strangely compliant. Everyone knew Salmik had begun as a pirate, but he never acted like one now. His armies didn't loot, or cause any unnecessary damage, or rape the local women, which was what everyone really expected them to do. The people kept their own languages, though they were expected to learn Gehunite as well. They kept most of their own customs. In effect, a country that was conquered and incorporated into the Empire remained very much as it had been, merely adding another layer to the bureaucracy, and bringing certain laws into compliance with Imperial law.

If there was slavery, it ended. The slave owners were compensated, and the slaves themselves aided in their transition to freedom. Perhaps ex-owner and ex-slave never quite became friends, but they learnt to tolerate each other, and after a generation or two it was not at all strange to find the families of owner and slave joined in marriage.

Gehun used its army and navy to conquer, but it used its diplomats to bind country and Empire into a single unit. It was an Empire of Nations, and each nation sent its representatives to the Imperial Parliament in Tufaria, now renamed Salmik, where the laws were made for everyone.

During this time of expansion, Salmik and Mira produced five children, two boys and three girls. The eldest, also called Mira, was born on the 11th day of Fourmonth, in the 6th year of the Empire. Crown Prince Udesh was next, born on the 19th day of Elevenmonth, in the 11th year of the Empire. Another daughter, Vonda, followed on 7th Fivemonth, 19, then Prince Felim, on 2nd Onemonth, 30, and the last, Sulae, born on New Year's Holiday, 31.

By the year 38, the Gehunite Empire had completely covered both North and South Gehun, for the continents had the same name as the country. Salmik was determined to add the far-flung Arzucaldan Empire to his domain. Ex-pirate or not, he had come to hate war, and sincerely felt that the best way to end it was for the entire world to be united as a single people.

His eldest son, Udesh, was killed on the first day of Twelvemonth in that year, during a naval engagement with an Arzucaldan sloop of war, *Prince Yachib*. Udesh's ship, *Invincible*, was captured and taken as a prize to Resh Bay, the Arzucaldan naval headquarters.

The war lasted seven years, and in the end little territory changed hands.

During the First Arzucaldan War, as it was called, Callaa had officially remained neutral, though the country had supplied a somewhat larger number of troops to Arzucalda, which was closer and still had a larger navy. At the end of the war, Crown Prince Felim was despatched to Callaahavn, Salmik wanting to reassure Queen Felia that he had no ill intent toward that tiny northern matriarchy.

In the event, during the visit Felim became acquainted with the queen's younger daughter, Geria, and the two decided to marry. Callaa would never become a part of the Empire, but the friendship between the two would never waver from that time forward.

IV
The Death of Salmik

War with Arzucalda was inadvertently renewed on 22nd Ninemonth, 48, when the Gehunite squadron carrying Crown Prince Felim on his fourth trip to Callaa—this time for the marriage, which had been delayed for several years because Queen Felia had been ill—was attacked by an Arzucaldan fleet enroute to Callaa with rather a more hostile intent.

The Gehunite squadron had picked up Alura Feliadaatin, the new Callaaite queen, who had been held prisoner in Arzucalda and only recently managed to escape.

The Gehunite squadron, though numerically inferior, employed new technology to win the battle. In those days, ships were armed with powerful, torsion powered throwing weapons, firing heavy iron darts and balls at the enemy. As naval weapons go, they were not that effective, and battles were decided by closing with the enemy and boarding them.

That changed on that day. The Gehunite flagship, HIMS *Foremost*, was commanded by Captain Galtor Romiwero, the son of Salmik's old first mate. Romiwero would later rise to vice admiral, and members of his family still serve right up to the present day. Romiwero had innovated new naval tactics, and, more importantly, had engineered a new weapon to implement those tactics.

When the small Gehunite fleet opened their ports on that day, what was presented to the enemy was not rows of cocked and loaded ballistas, but dark rows of black iron tubes that roared and spit fire and smoke and heavy metal balls that could smash a ship's timbers from well outside ballista range. In a secret project conducted on a remote island on the Gulf side of the Gehunite peninsula, Romiwero and his engineers had invented the first naval guns.

The Gehunite fleet continued to Callaahavn, where Felim and Geria were duly married. Queen Alura hardly outlived her mother, dying on 28th Tenmonth, 48, and Geria ascended the throne, her elder sister having left no children. It was during this time that Felim received news that his father had died of a heart attack on 19th Eightmonth, making him the new emperor.

His wife promptly abdicated in favour of her sister, Felia, at that time still a toddler. Though her marriage to Felim could have served to unite the two countries, popular sentiment was for continued independence, so she would become Empress Consort of Gehun, and her sister Queen Felia VIII of Gehun. Queen Alura's widowed husband, Prince Horik, would serve as regent until Felia was 15 and came of age.

This, then, is the story of the founding of our Empire, and of the demigod who was our first emperor. It may seem a bit fantastic today, nearly four centuries after the events, yet our chronicles assure us it is true.

There is much more to tell, but that, as it is said, is another story.

MORT'S MAID

[Writing as Jacob Thomson]

There were times when I really envied my cousin Mort. He was the wealthy one in the family, living in a big house a couple of miles outside town. People sometimes say that so-and-so lives on an "estate," but in Mort's case it was literally true. His house, which was enormous, sat right in the middle of a 35-acre plot. The land was cleared to a distance of some 500 feet around the house, and carefully manicured and landscaped. The rest was virgin forest, with many trees rising over 100 feet.

None of us ever really understood how Mort managed to keep the place up. The house—well, mansion, really—contained 28 rooms. Mort was the only guy I ever knew who lived in a house with an actual drawing room. He also had a library, a private study, a gun room, both formal and informal dining rooms, living room, parlor, a commercial kitchen, butler's pantry, a TV room with a giant screen set and theatre seating for 20, and an even dozen bedrooms, each with its own private bath.

Naturally, there were servants' quarters. You couldn't keep up a place like that without servants, or so you'd think. And that's where it was odd. When the house was built, back in the late 19th Century, there had been a butler, a cook, two footmen, and five maids to take care of the inside of the house. There was also a full time gardener to take care of the grounds. A couple of grooms and a coachman, who had their own quarters over the old coach house, had completed the household staff.

That was then. But now Mort had only a single servant, who presumably did everything. He had a maid. She was a small woman, no more than three inches over five feet tall, and utterly perfect. She was slim where she should be slim and curved where she should be curved. Though I never saw her except in her uniform—the traditional black dress, with lace collar and apron—I was sure her figure had to be perfect.

She was also remarkably beautiful, presently wearing her long, black hair gathered at the back of her head. The only odd thing was that she always wore rather long bangs, nearly covering her forehead down to her eyebrows. I saw her hair in a number of styles over the years, but the bangs were a constant.

And she never seemed to get any older. When I first encountered her, during a visit shortly after my 22nd birthday, she appeared to be in her mid twenties. I just turned 53 a few months ago, and when she answered the door to admit me this morning she still looked exactly the same as when I had first met her some 31 years before.

"You have a picture up in the attic that's getting older, don't you, Yvette?" I commented.

She smiled and beckoned for me to enter, but said nothing. She never did. As Mort explained it, she was like Don Diego's servant, able to hear normally, but for some unexplainable reason unable to speak.

Not that I cared. She was young and beautiful, and I was rapidly turning into an old geezer who appreciated young, beautiful women more and more as the years passed. The sad part was that, as the years went by, they appreciated me less and less. Such is life, I suppose.

Yvette led me into the gun room, indicating a chair by the window. She gestured out the window, and following her pointing finger I could just see Mort stalking along the edge of the forest, a pair of powerful binoculars and a long-lensed camera hanging around his neck. Mort was an avid amateur ornithologist—a bird watcher.

It was one of his hobbies, of which he had many.

His hobbies were his occupation. No one in the family knew exactly how much money Mort had, but it was obvious that he had more than enough. A local real estate agent had just told me that Mort's house and grounds were the object of a developer's attention, and that he had been offered seven million for the place. In the agent's opinion, the offer was a little on the low side, but not by much.

The developer wanted the place for a shopping mall. Mort wasn't interested in selling, and that was where it stood, much to the annoyance of the agent, who stood to make close to half a million dollars in commission if the deal went through.

"Your cousin should probably reconsider," he'd told me. "These guys want the land, and I don't think they're used to people turning them down. I'm a little concerned for him."

"How long have you known Mort?" I'd asked.

"Maybe 40 years. I sold him that place, way back when I was just getting started in this business.

"Then you know he probably won't sell. He never leaves his estate. Anything he needs, he just has delivered. I think the only way you'll ever get him out of there is when he's dead. Maybe not even then. He's got a private mausoleum behind the house, presuming the county will allow him to use it."

"I know," the agent said, shaking his head. "That's the problem. I get the feeling the guys backing this shopping mall deal are the type who might be inclined to arrange it if he's too stubborn. And the county won't let him be buried there, either. He'd have to subdivide the land and set aside a minimum of ten acres as a cemetery to do it."

This was one reason I was out at Mort's house today. Mort was a stubborn old guy, but he might not know just who he was dealing with. The agent never said, exactly, but there was a strong impression the developer was some sort of Mob front.

Well, for the moment, I was sitting in a very comfortable chair, sometimes looking out the window, and sometimes watching Yvette as she dusted the dead animals. There were heads all over the walls, and several full body mounts scattered around the room, with gun cases in between. The room had always struck me as rather an odd place. We're Jewish, and Jews don't hunt. I don't think it's any particular Jewish repugnance at killing game animals, mind you. It's just that, the way we're taught, if you shoot an animal the meat isn't kosher, so what's the point?

The family who built the house, of course, were gentiles, and had obviously hunted on several continents. When Mort bought the house the furnishings, including the mounted trophies and guns, came with it. The original builder's family had withered away and died, leaving only a nephew who lived in California and didn't care about the old family place, which he hadn't seen since he was three. Mort made an offer for the estate and the nephew took it.

After a while, Yvette finished her dusting and left the gun room. I continued to look out the window. This room was a favorite of Mort's, but I'd never cared for it. You can recognize that hunting is a part of the natural order, man simply being another predator and every bit as much a part of nature as a wolf or cougar, but that doesn't mean you may not have philosophical objections. I'd never been placed in a position where I had to take a life. At least, nothing higher in the natural order than the random insect. I wasn't sure I could. I doubted that actual hunting was in Mort's nature, either. But he kept the old trophies.

I honestly wondered just how much of the house really reflected Mort's personality, and how much was simply preserved, like a museum, from the original occupants. The library often seemed to me to be the only room where you could really see the current owner. The shelves were crowded with his books, some of them very old.

My cousin was a curious man. He wasn't in the least religious, probably hadn't been inside a synagogue in the last 20 years, yet he was as well versed in Jewish law and tradition as any rabbi. Mort could cite the entire Babylonian Talmud from memory. I've tested him on this, giving him what I was sure were a number of extremely obscure passages. He could not only tell me which volume they were from, but cite the page, column and line, and rattle off every commentary on the citation.

His passion was Cabala. I doubt there was a single book, text, or treatise on the subject, no matter how obscure, he didn't own. But he had no interest at all in what he called "Pop Cabala," the sort of thing being taught to celebrities. He was quite sure it was all just another fad and, in any case, even the deepest popular teachings were, in his estimation, no more than a very superficial treatment.

"They teach this stuff to children," he'd told me. "How deeply can they be delving? You can't teach Cabala, real Cabala, to children. The rules are quite clear on that. Before you may begin to learn in Cabala you must be at least 40 years old, and have a very thorough knowledge of every aspect of Jewish law and tradition. If you lack those prerequisites, you'll never really be able to learn, and you may very well end up going crazy instead."

Mind you, I've never really understood any of it. Mort claimed that Cabala could explain the workings of the Universe. I was more inclined to look to science. I suppose this is why Mort is a wealthy, eccentric artist and philosopher and I'm a civil engineer.

While I was mulling this over, Mort returned to the house. Coming into the gun room, he greeted me, then walked across the room to one of the gun cabinets, putting his binoculars and camera in a drawer in the lower section.

"I hope you haven't been too bored, David," Mort said. "If I'd known you were coming out here I wouldn't have been wandering about in the woods looking for birds."

"I was okay. Yvette was dusting in here. That was actually sort of entertaining to watch."

"She is a beauty, isn't she?" He smiled.

"That she is. Almost too beautiful. She has to be close to 60, but hardly looks older than her middle twenties."

"She will be 64 in three months," Mort replied. "But I never intended her to age, so she remains young."

This was new. It wasn't the first time I'd noticed that Yvette seemed frozen at about 24, but this was the first time I'd heard Mort say anything implying he might have something to do with her perpetual youthfulness.

"What do you have to do with it?"

"Learn your Cabala, David, and you'll understand."

"What does the Cabala have to do with people not getting older?"

"Nothing at all."

That made about as much sense as most of Mort's cabalistic musings, which was none at all. If the Cabala had nothing to do with people not aging, then why would I understand the phenomenon if I studied it? Ask me why a delicate looking bridge can carry a pair of fully-loaded freight trains at the same time without falling down, or how many cubic yards of concrete are needed for a 200 foot tall dam, and I can give you an answer. A direct answer, not one that seems to rely on circular logic with a huge hole in the circle.

Yvette came back into the gun room, nodding to Mort. "Supper," he said. "You'll stay, won't you, David?"

"Of course."

Yvette was also the cook. One of the best in the world, in my opinion, and I've traveled enough to know. In any case, I'd come out here to talk to Mort about the possible threat from the mall developers. Probably not a subject for the table, but certainly appropriate afterward.

The meal was, as expected, excellent. Chicken, prepared with some sort of herb coating and deep fried. There was a choice of green beans or peas—I took both—and whipped potatoes with real butter. (We don't actually keep kosher in our family, obviously.) A bottle of wine from Mort's extensive cellars completed the meal. For some reason he never serves desserts, so I'd long ago learned not to expect them.

Our stomachs full, we retired to the library to talk. "You know," I said, "Jim Curtis thinks you may be in some danger."

Mort leaned back in his chair. "Jim wants his commission on this place. I have no plans to sell. I like it here."

"He seems to think the people who want to buy your property are Mob types."

"I had them checked out," Mort said. "Jim is correct."

"That doesn't bother you?"

"Not much. Does it bother you?"

"I'd like to keep you around a while longer. How many relatives do we have left?"

Mort got up and walked to a bookcase, pulling a small, leather-bound volume from the shelf. He flipped through the pages, read something, and replaced the book on the shelf before resuming his seat.

"In answer to your question, David, I have exactly one living relative, and that would be you. I'm going to be 88 next year, which means I have already outlived the oldest previously known member of our family by 20 years. We tend to die fairly young, in case you haven't noticed. If these gangsters kill me, well, this estate will be your problem then."

"I don't want it. Not anytime soon, at least."

"Don't worry. I'm in no hurry to pass it on."

Yvette came in just then, a quizzical look on her lovely face. "I think we won't be needing you for the rest of the evening, Yvette," Mort told her.

She nodded and went out, her footsteps retreating toward the back of the house, where the servants' quarters were located. She had quite a spacious apartment for herself back there, having full use of a space originally built to house a complete live-in staff.

"I still think you might want to take some precautions," I said. "This house is pretty isolated, sitting in the middle of all this land with no close neighbors."

"What sort of precautions? Hire bodyguards? They'd just get in the way." He smiled. "Besides, I have Yvette, don't I?"

"What kind of protection can she provide? She's just a woman, and a rather tiny one at that. Do you think she'll charm the bad guys into leaving you alone?"

"She's more capable than you might think. A very tough customer, as we used to say. Perhaps she could charm them with her beauty, but she could also take more direct action."

I shook my head. "You mean, she's some sort of karate expert or something?"

"Nothing of the sort. I'd just say that anyone who tried to take her on might be in for quite a surprise."

I could see I was getting nowhere and, as it was getting dark, I decided to head for home. Mort walked with me to the front door, still reassuring me that he was in no danger. I had a feeling he was wrong, but knew I'd never be able to convince him. He had to come to that conclusion on his own.

I was a quarter mile down the road when a big Lincoln, with out of state plates, passed me going the other direction. I didn't think anything of it at first, until I saw the turn signals come on and the car make a left turn. There were no roads back there, only Mort's long, winding drive.

Mort almost never had visitors, with the exception of me, and some delivery people. It was too late for deliveries and, in any case, I couldn't think of anything you delivered in a Lincoln, other than possibly unwelcome guests. But he clearly had visitors now. Just as clearly, he hadn't been expecting them, or he would certainly have said something.

I turned the car around and drove back to the estate. The Lincoln was parked by the main door. As I was shutting off the engine I heard a single, muffled "crack!" from the house, and there was a flash in the drawing room window. Acting foolish, as people frequently do in that sort of situation, I ran into the house and hurried down the hall.

Mort was standing by the fireplace, still holding the poker in his right hand. He looked at me and smiled weakly. "I told you it would be all right," he said.

It didn't look all right to me. There were three bodies sprawled on the floor, two rather large men, wearing black suits, and Yvette. All three were obviously dead. One man had the front of his head stove in, bearing the imprint of the mantelpiece. The other had a long crease in the back of his skull, which I had no doubt would match the poker in Mort's hand. There were two pistols on the floor near the men.

Yvette lay face down on the parquet floor. There could be no question she was dead, even without turning her over. She was still in her uniform, the skirt hiked up in back, exposing most of her legs. She was gray, and a very unnatural gray at that. Clearly there was no blood flowing through her veins.

"Have you called the police?" I asked.

"In a minute. I need to take care of Yvette first."

"I think she's dead, Mort. You shouldn't move her. The police will want to see this scene exactly the way it is."

Mort smiled and knelt beside the maid, rolling her over onto her back. "She'll be fine," he said.

He brushed back her bangs with his hand. Curiously, the hair had become stiff, so that it stayed where he moved it, standing up from her head. More curiously, I now noticed that her hair had turned the same odd gray color as her body. There was a deep crease across her forehead where a bullet had hit her. There was no blood, which I didn't understand. Nor did I understand what appeared to be the Hebrew letters *Mem* and *Sov*, seemingly incised into her forehead. It was no wonder she always wore those bangs, I thought, for they would hide the scars.

Mort looked up at me. "Easily fixed," he said.

"Easily fixed?"

"David, you remember how I made my money, don't you?"

"Sure. You're an artist. A painter and a sculptor."

"Well, then, you can see that this is no great problem. With his finger he smoothed the crease in Yvette's forehead. It all came together neatly, more like clay than flesh. "You know what the word *meis* means, don't you?"

I nodded. The Hebrew letters on her forehead. "It means 'death'," I said.

"Precisely. But if you put an *alef* in front of it, then it becomes 'emes,' which means 'truth'." He took his PDA from his pocket and took out the stylus. "This should do," he said.

He took the stylus and incised an *alef* into Yvette's forehead. "*Alef*, you remember, is not only a letter, it is also the number one. One is the most basic attribute of God, as it declares in the Torah, 'Hear, O Israel, the Lord is our God, the Lord is One.' And *emes*, truth, without God in it is no truth at all, but death. But, if we restore God, then it becomes true again, doesn't it?"

Yvette opened her eyes. What I saw, as the lids opened, were not eyes, but only the sculpted images of them in gray clay. But, as I watched, the color returned to her skin, her eyes again took on the appearance of normality, and her hair returned to its usual black. Mort helped her to her feet. "Now," he said, "we will call the police."

I really couldn't help much when the police arrived. I had still been parking my car when the shot was fired. As Mort explained it, when the gangsters broke in to attack him, Yvette had shoved one of them into the mantelpiece, instantly killing him. The other had gone after her, firing one shot and missing, and Mort had grabbed the poker and killed him. The explanation satisfied the detectives, and after a few hours the bodies were taken away. The police asked us to stay out of the drawing room for a while, until they were sure the forensic people had been able to collect any physical evidence, but they left us in no doubt that they considered the whole thing justifiable and that no charges were likely to be filed.

After the police had left, the three of us were sitting in the library. "I don't think we'll have any more trouble, do you?" Mort said.

"Probably not. But you know, you lied to the police."

"Not in any way that would change things."

"You said the second guy fired and missed. He didn't miss. We both know that."

"Of course. But I could hardly tell the detectives that, could I? What would they think? They'd probably lock me up as some sort of nut."

"I'm not sure I really believe any of this myself."

"And there's the problem. You're Jewish, you've heard all the old legends, and you don't believe it. How well do you think I'd fare with a Christian cop? 'Well, officer, he killed my maid, but that was okay, because I sculpted her out of clay myself about 64 years ago, so I knew how to fix her.' I don't think he'd consider it credible." He smiled. "After all, how many cops have even heard of a *golem?*"

PREDATOR

[Writing as Jacob Thomson]

He thought of himself as a predator. In nature, predation was an important part of the ecological system. Predators removed the animals who could no longer keep up with the herd. They culled the weak, the sick, the unfit specimens that needed to be removed from the gene pool for the benefit of the others.

Nature wasn't a cartoon, he thought. The cute little animals didn't spend their days frolicking in a bright, sunny meadow. Mostly, he thought, a lot of them spent the day eating grass, or twigs, or other vegetation, while the rest spent the day killing and eating the herbivores. It was all a part of the natural balance, and if you left it alone it usually worked out for the best.

At least, for the best in an overall sense. It was obviously hard on the individual deer or rabbit that found itself as a predator's supper. But it was good for the majority of those who didn't.

That was one of the problems with people, he thought. They had done too much in the way of tampering with the natural balance. If a child was born it had something like a 96% chance of surviving to adulthood, and nearly as good a chance of reproducing.

And this was true both of the superior individuals, whose progeny could be expected to contribute the most to the collective good of humanity, and of the sickly and weak, who could probably contribute best by not reproducing at all.

Curiously, he had never taken this idea to the usual conclusion. He wasn't a racist. It had never once occurred to him that a particular race was superior. Strong, healthy individuals of any race were included in his definition of superior. The same was true when he classified the inferior.

The problem, to his way of thinking, was that too many of the wrong people were growing up and having inferior children. In earlier times, when the human race was steadily progressing, slightly more than half of all children could be expected to die before they were two. It was nature's way of culling the weak and inferior before they were old enough to mate and pass on their bad genes.

But this no longer happened, which left it up to him. He knew, as surely as he was alive, that this was the reason he had been created and placed on the earth.

Now, he didn't hurt children. It wasn't their fault, really, that modern medicine was extending their lives past the point where nature should have removed them from the gene pool. Instead, he culled the inferior adults. Mostly, he hoped, *before* they could reproduce.

He had an inborn gift for finding these people. He could tell just by looking at someone whether they deserved to live or die. He wasn't sure how he knew—he just did. How did the wolf know which caribou needed to be culled from the herd? It was an instinct; something that simply was.

He never thought it odd that all of the inferior specimens he culled were women. Again, this was simply something that just was. He had nothing against women in general. He merely had a talent for recognizing the ones who needed to be removed from the gene pool. He thought there were probably men who also needed culling, but he hadn't found any of them yet.

He had managed to discover 28 women so far. They were all dead now, of course. After all, what was the value of these insights into the natural order if he didn't follow up on them? Once he recognized that a woman needed to be removed, it became his duty to nature to remove her.

He wasn't sure just how he knew. It wasn't anything obvious. Most of them had looked normal enough—even healthy and attractive. But he knew that an outward appearance of good health could conceal the truth; that her genes were bad, and that she would produce more weak, useless children to further drag down the quality of the human race.

This knowledge came to him from some instinctive source. He could look at any woman and know if she was supposed to live or die. On this single topic, his judgment was never wrong. Every woman he believed should die did die. So he had to be right. Otherwise, they would easily have defended themselves, and would still be alive.

It was a basic law of nature that the fit would always survive. If they didn't, they obviously didn't deserve to.

Just now he was searching. It was never ending, this mission he had set for himself. He had to go out each night, looking at every person he encountered, waiting for that intuitive recognition of the inferior that would set him on the trail of yet another genetic misprint in need of erasure.

Most of the people he encountered this night were just fine. There was nothing about them crying out to his instincts, alerting him that something needed to be done. It was like that most nights. He would prowl the city and no one would draw his interest.

But some nights it was different. On those nights he would notice a particular woman, and something deep in his highly-developed brain would instantly identify her as one of the bad ones. He might not do anything that night, but he would remember her.

Once he knew where she lived, the rest was easy enough. At some point he would get into her home, or catch her in a place where there was no danger of being disturbed. If she was unmarried, and not involved with anyone, he might take longer. If she had a husband, though, he felt compelled to work more quickly. She might get pregnant and, as his purpose was to prevent any more genetically inferior children from being born, it was important to remove her from the gene pool as expeditiously as possible.

The girl walking ahead of him caught his eye. She was tall and slender, dressed in a sheath skirt and a white, fitted blouse. Physically, she was a wonderful specimen, with a perfect figure, good legs, and long, shiny hair in a striking coppery red color.

But she was also one of them. His instincts were screaming at him, warning him that, beautiful as this girl might be, she was one of the genetic defectives, and should not be allowed to live long enough to pass on her imperfect genes to the next generation.

Of course, the knowledge that he would have to kill her didn't preclude having a little fun at the same time. That was one of the privileges of his special position in nature's genetic enforcement corps. Should he so choose, he was allowed to have sex with the women before killing them.

His own genes were, obviously, superior, and so should be combined only with the genes of an equally superior woman when it was time to reproduce. Still, as the defective women would die once he'd had them, it didn't matter. They would serve the useful function of giving him pleasure before they died.

Like this one, he thought. She was turning into an alley now, probably taking a short cut over to the next avenue. All the better for him. He wondered if that was what he had recognized in her, that she was one who would take foolish chances. She was making it easy on him. He could simply follow her down the alley, take her in the darkness, and then kill her right there.

He knew the city in every detail. There was a narrow side alley about halfway along the wider alley, between an old theatre on one side and the back of a row of three-story retail buildings on the other. You couldn't see into that side alley from either main street. It was a perfect venue for what he had in mind.

He quickly glanced around, pleased to discover that he was virtually alone on the street. With another quick look back he slipped into the alley.

The girl was about 50 feet in front of him, strolling toward the next street as if she hadn't a care in the world.

He always tried to move quietly, but this time it was as if she simply wasn't listening. He caught up with her just as she was passing the side alley and swiftly dragged her into it, his hand clasped tightly over her mouth to prevent her crying out. She hardly seemed to resist, and in a moment he had her pushed up against the back of the old theatre's loading dock. Soon, he thought, there would be one more misfit removed from the gene pool.

But she was fighting back now. He was a big man, three inches over six feet tall, weighing 225 pounds and hardly an ounce of fat on his well-muscled body. Yet the girl was pushing him away, catching hold of his wrists and wrenching them from her lithe body, the effort hardly showing on her lovely face.

"You're not very smart, are you?" she said. Her tone was flat, dismissive. "Why so rough? I hate it when men act like brutes."

He couldn't believe it. Despite his size, the girl was pushing him back, forcing him up against the opposite wall, his arms pinned at his sides as she leaned toward him, her lips inches from his.

"Foolish," she said. "It didn't have to be like this."

She leaned forward, her lips lightly brushing his cheek. His mind was reeling. Was she coming on to him? He felt her kissing him, her soft lips against his throat, the tip of her tongue flicking out against the sensitive skin.

There was hardly any pain at all. He felt a slight pressure on his throat, a sharp twinge as the girl's canine teeth pierced the skin and plunged into the artery beneath. But it didn't really hurt, even as the world began to fade, and the only sound was the frantic pumping of his heart.

Five minutes later the girl walked out of the alley and turned east on the broad sidewalk. It had been easier than she'd expected, and curiously satisfying. She didn't think she was a bad person, after all. It was just her nature. And this time, in this man, she had sensed true evil. A predator, he thought of himself. She had sensed that, taken in his thoughts with his blood.

But he was, after all, only an amateur. One who killed from some psychotic delusion, not out of necessity. A mere child. And he had forgotten the most basic rule of predation. That predators come in all sizes. Foxes ate rabbits, but coyotes ate foxes, and cougars ate coyotes. And there was always a bigger fish. How was he to know that his intended prey was by far the more experienced predator?

You could learn a lot about your craft, she thought, when you'd been at it for more than seven centuries.

A PATIENT MAN
[Writing as Jacob Thomson]

I am a very patient man. When I have set my mind on a goal, I do not feel it must be accomplished instantly. There is always plenty of time to act. Haste makes waste, the saying goes, and I quite agree.

So it was in the matter of Felder. I was patient, Felder was not. This, I knew, was why I would triumph in the end. Oh, there was many a time I thought of just what I should do with Felder. He was a most annoying young man, conceited, very full of himself.

As why shouldn't he be? He was quite wealthy, and my employer's son. They say the apple doesn't fall far from the tree, but in Felder's case I must say that it dropped and rolled a good, long distance before coming to rest. His father was a true gentleman, kind, generous, slow to anger and quick to forgive. Precisely the opposite of his son, who merely assumed a genial façade, but beneath the surface was utterly selfish and uncaring for his fellow man.

Now, I always held his father in high regard. This is one reason I felt that patience was called for. Harming Felder would no doubt have grieved his father, and I did not wish for that to happen. But, still, Felder himself deserved nothing good. More than once I found myself thinking of inviting him down into the deepest cellar for a nice glass of amontillado, then walling him up to scream his life out in darkness.

I never did that, of course. Felder would never fall for the trick, and I didn't have a capacious wine cellar in which to wall him up. A few dozen bottles of cheap wine in the closet, and even those cheap wines, the best the local discount grocer had to offer, were in any case too good for Felder.

Nor could I take a cue from the Brewster sisters, give him a nice glass of home made elderberry wine laced with cyanide and "just a pinch of strychnine," though burying his body in the cellar—that cellar again—did have its appeal.

I had so many thoughts over the years as I plotted my revenge. Felder dropped from a factory catwalk into a vat of acid, or a ladle of molten steel. Felder tied to the railroad tracks, with the 6:10 right on time. Felder tied to a log and run very slowly through a saw mill, feet first, in order to increase and prolong the pain. Felder introduced to a beautiful demure young lady, whose casual wear, once they were alone, would prove to be mostly leather and steel spikes, and who would take great pleasure in slowly dismembering such an obnoxious specimen.

But I did none of this. How could I? Even if I wasn't caught, and in our fantasies we never are, any harm done to Felder would cause grief to his father, and his father was my employer, my mentor, and my friend.

Now, as I said before, I am a patient man. Patience is usually rewarded. The day came when Felder's father passed away. Felder himself was not particularly upset, for with his father's passing he gained a controlling interest in the business. His two sisters, however, were distraught not only at their father's passing, but at what their odious brother intended to do. You see, Felder had plans. Once his father was safely in his grave, he intended to sell out to a big chain.

"Family operated funeral homes," he declared, "are obsolete." Adding, to me, "If you're lucky, maybe the new owners will let you keep your job. If not, it hardly matters, does it? You're an old man and you should be thinking about retiring."

I had no interest in retiring. My job wasn't particularly hard, after all, and my customers never complained. As for my customer's families, well, most were quite happy to see how good their departed relative looked in his casket. I am a bit of an artist. Most of my customers went into the ground looking better than they did during their final years.

So did my employer. I took particular care with him, and I was properly sad at the funeral. Why not? I liked the old man, and he had always been good to me. It was his son, his odious son, who had made my life hell.

Felder didn't even show up for his father's funeral. Neither of his sisters seemed particularly surprised, and both presumed he was either off negotiating the sale of their father's funeral home or patronizing some streetwalker.

When several weeks had passed, and Felder did not reappear, things began to settle down. The police had been notified the day after the funeral, but they had made no progress. It was as if the detestable Felder had simply walked right off the face of the earth. The sisters, who were less venial and much more like their father, continued to refuse all offers from the big chains.

After three years, and still no sign of their brother, the sisters decided to change the name of the business from "Felder & Son" to "Felder & Nichols," taking me in as a full partner. I knew the business and did most of the work, after all. No one knew what would happen if Felder suddenly decided to reappear, but we continued to run the place, by now hoping he would not.

But now, patient as I am, I believe the time has come. My doctor has been in for the final time today, and has admitted that I can hardly expect to live through the night. That is why I have decided to tell this story. For the truth is, I know where Felder is. I know precisely where he has been for all these years and where, I presume, he will remain.

Felder's father was a very large man, six and half feet tall, and weighing nearly 350 pounds. Felder himself was a runt, only 5' 3", and he weighed, I should think, no more than 130 pounds.

A man like Felder's father has to be buried in a special casket, much larger than the standard models. A solid bronze oversize casket like the one we used is quite heavy, even without the deceased resting inside. So no one noticed that this one was, perhaps, a little heavier than it should have been, nor did they hear the faint sounds of drugged breathing from beneath the thin mattress on the adjustable platform supporting the body.

I still wonder what Felder thought when the drugs finally wore off and he awakened in the low, narrow space at the bottom of the casket. Did he scream? Did he plead for his life? Did he try to claw his way out? I can only speculate, for by that time the casket was tucked away inside its concrete vault and covered over with four feet of earth. If he screamed, no one could hear him.

If I am patient, Felder was not. But I do have to wonder if he finally learned patience. It wasn't as if there was anything else for him to do.

CASTLE GROSSHELM
[Writing as Jacob Thomson]

Naught but scattered rubble remains upon the ancient hill, where antique stones here and there thrust up through the bare earth. Black soil, rich and fertile appearing, yet strangely barren. Around the hill lies a vast, virgin forest, with here and there an ancient wagon track, or a peasant's small hut and garden, the blue-gray smoke rising from the chimney. The forest ends perhaps halfway up the slope of the hill, turning to a lovely green meadow, sprinkled in summer with wildflowers.

But the crest is barren. Where once an ancient castle keep rose to challenge the sky, surrounded by a tall, crenelated wall, there is now only rubble and the rich black loam that should support luxuriant greenery, but where nothing at all will grow. Grass seed had been scattered there, and the summer flower seeds, carried on the breeze, fell into the soil and there they died.

The local peasants never venture more than a few yards above the tree line, and never after dark. No one can remember when the castle still dominated the hill. There is only a story, generations old, of how a strange plague slowly wiped out the noble family who dwelt in that place, until the last had been carried down the winding stairs and laid to rest in the venerable crypt buried deep in the bedrock of the hill, and the castle was left to the elements.

More generations passed, and the wind and rain broke through the castle roof, until the floors collapsed into the lowest levels and only the crumbling wall remained. And then, just after the beginning of the 19th Century, a fire had swept through the tumbled beams and boards piled up inside the keep and the heat had finished the work of centuries and the ancient edifice collapsed in upon itself.

The outer curtain wall had long ago succumbed to the need for building stone. It was said that there was hardly a house in the district that did not have at least a few of its stones built into a foundation or wall. With the fire having tumbled the keep, those stones, as well, slowly vanished from the site, to be incorporated into some newer structure. At last, only those half buried stones that remain today were left, marking the burial site of the ancient Von Grosshelm family, whose name was memorialized only in the memories of the oldest peasants, for the great stone lintel of the burial crypt, where it was chiseled deep in the hard granite, was itself buried deep beneath the earth and rubble and out of sight of modern man.

And so it remained until the 1950s, when an avaricious government became aware of the stories of great wealth buried along with the corpses in the Von Grosshelm crypt. There was gold there, it was said, gold in great abundance. Chests of old coins, and rich religious treasure in the tiny chapel at the entrance to the crypt. It seemed strange even to the supposedly benevolent men in Bucharest that no one had plundered the crypt ages ago, but the story was that a fear of the plague breaking out again kept the locals away, and men from farther away had never heard the stories.

So men were brought to the hill to excavate. Ragged men, still dressed in the tattered remains of the field gray uniforms they had been captured in back in 1945. Men brought from prison camps in Siberia, who knew they were never going to return home. They had suffered the misfortune of being captured by the Red Army, and the Soviet Union was not so forgiving as the western powers. Prisoners must be made to pay for the crimes of their government, and for the crimes they had committed themselves, even if those crimes were no more than an administrative excuse to make slaves of a former enemy's troops.

It was doubly hard, this grueling work of excavating the ruined castle, for the prisoners knew they were only a few hundred miles from Germany—closer than they had been since the day they marched off to the east in expectation of a short campaign and an easy victory. Nor did the knowledge of the place they were digging help, for Grosshelm is a German name, meaning "great helmet," and no doubt adopted in honor of some ancient knight's oversized jousting helm. They were digging up the tomb of one of the old Teutonic overlords of this country, perhaps even the grave of a distant relative. Coming of age in the ardently nationalistic Hitlerian years, where the old Teutonic Knights were given the awe and veneration of national demigods, such an act seemed little short of sacrilege.

The Russian guards, who had no great love of their socialist comrades in Bucharest, fenced off the perimeter of the hill twenty meters above the tree line. The fence, made of barbed wire, served a dual purpose. It functioned both to keep the prisoners in, and to keep the Romanians out.

If greed in Bucharest had prompted the excavation of Castle Grosshelm, an even greater greed in Moscow was determined to insure that any wealth found made its way back to the Kremlin, and to hell with the Romanians.

It was slow work. Moscow had provided the prisoners and the guards, but they had not provided proper equipment. The workers were given shovels, long pry bars, picks and other hand tools, but there were no cranes or steam shovels or bulldozers. Each of the massive stones had to be dug out, then pried from its place and somehow dragged or carried away by the prisoners. What a properly equipped work force could have done in a week dragged on for nearly a year before the prisoners at last unearthed the top of a rubble filled stairway leading down into the living rock.

Even then, four more weeks passed before the rubble was laboriously hauled up and the full depth of the stairway exposed. At the bottom, a broad landing connected the stair with the chapel entrance, where a massive, iron-bound door, locked tight, barred entry.

The Russian officer in charge of the working party was momentarily stymied. Before the war he had been trained as an art historian, and his first thought was that the chapel door itself was part of the vanished castle's treasure. The wooden panels were heavily carved with religious figures. In the capitalist world, he thought, the door would be worth thousands of dollars. Comrade Stalin, he decided, would not appreciate it if he simply put his men to work breaking it down.

But it was hinged on the inside, so neither could he knock the pins out of the hinges and remove the door from the frame. "I don't suppose," he said, "that any of you men was a locksmith—or a burglar?"

One of the prisoners had been a locksmith in civilian life, but the Russians had never been told that bit of information and he wasn't about to volunteer it now. There were German dead inside the vault beyond the chapel, and he would do nothing extra to help the Russian steal from them.

The prisoners were herded back to the surface. A soldier was sent to the village for a locksmith, but returned an hour later with the news that none was to be found. If the lieutenant needed a locksmith, he would have to send to Bucharest. The village was so poor that, having nothing for anyone to steal, the peasants had no real locks on their doors.

The lieutenant decided he would attempt other methods. A cold chisel and hammer were procured and one of the prisoners was put to work cutting the rivet heads off the thick iron lockplate. The lock was two or three centuries old, at least, he reasoned, so it was probably a fairly simple warded type that could be easily defeated as long as he could get to the guts. Cutting off the rivet heads, he thought, should not cause irreparable damage.

This proved to be the case, and at last the massive door swung into the chapel. The officer entered first, shining his flashlight around the interior. The room was square, about twenty feet on each side and topped by a barrel-vaulted ceiling. The entry door was on the east side, or so the lieutenant believed—his compass wouldn't work inside the mountain, and the stair changed directions several times on the way down.

There was an elaborate altar against the northern wall, covered by a gold brocade altar cloth. A tall, gold crucifix was at the center of the altar, flanked by a pair of four-branched gold candelabra, the candles still in them. In the center of the chapel, in front of the altar, was a long, stone catafalque, where a coffin would rest during a committal service, before being taken into the burial vault.

The entrance to the vault was in the west wall, a tall, gothic arched opening, blocked by a wrought iron gate. There was a short marble column placed directly in front of the gate, with another, even larger, gold crucifix resting on its flat top.

"Collect all of this and take it to the top," the lieutenant ordered. "I will record each piece as it is removed," he added, "just in case one of you might be thinking of stealing something."

Despite having had the poor judgment to serve in the army of a tyrant, the prisoners were all honest men. So far as they were concerned, the only thief was the Soviet government that was looting the chapel and tomb.

It was nearly dark by the time the last of the loot was removed from the chapel. The Russian officer decided that enough had been accomplished for one day. He would worry about getting through the gate, and to any treasure in the burial vault, in the morning.

*   *   *

Dieter Krause jerked awake to the staccato sound of a guard's Kalashnikov on full automatic. A moment later the shooting stopped, followed instantly by a terrified scream that was itself shut off as if someone had slammed a door on the source.

Around him, Krause could see the other prisoners also sitting upright on their cots, peering about in the dim light that filtered through the canvas walls and roof of their leaky tent. He motioned for them to remain silent and cautiously got to his feet. Before he was captured, Krause had been a captain of infantry, and he was now the highest ranking prisoner in the group. They all wanted to know what was going on, but it was his place to take the risk of peeking through the tent's door. The Prussian sense of duty and leadership was still there.

He wouldn't dare go into the floodlit compound. The Russians had made it quite clear that leaving the tent after lights out would be instantly punished by shooting the transgressor. He could only peek through the canvas flap and hope no one noticed.

Cautiously, he moved the flap to one side, opening a narrow slit sufficient to peer through with one eye. Just inside the main gate a guard opened fire, shooting at something moving along the barbed wire fence. Another figure appeared from the opposite direction, moving swiftly up behind the guard. The figure was clearly not a prisoner, for even from his vantage point Krause could see the slim, white form covered by a flowing gown, and the long, black hair flowing down her back.

The mysterious girl was within inches of the guard before he realized anyone was behind him. Her arm slipped around his chest, lifting him off his feet, and then she slammed him to the ground. The girl knelt over him. Another figure, this time clearly male and dressed in a costume that seemed out of a Renaissance movie, rushed in from the direction where the guard had been firing. Like the girl, he knelt over the fallen guard.

At that moment Krause's view was abruptly blocked by a face. The man standing before the tent was tall and gaunt, his narrow face framed by flowing white hair, worn in a fashion that had gone out of style centuries before. His eyes were deep set, dark as midnight. But it was his mouth that riveted Krause's attention.

The man's lips were thin, his mouth partly open, revealing a line of unusually white teeth. The lower lip was slightly distended, and there was fresh blood dripping down his long chin.

"Himmel!"

The man looked closer at the single eye peering out at him. *"Deutscher?"* he said.

"Ja." Krause could hardly speak. He had gone to sleep a prisoner and somehow awakened in a horror movie.

"Why are you here?" the man asked, his German oddly accented and curiously phrased, sounding like some of the old books Krause had studied in University.

"We are war prisoners," he managed to say.

"Working for these Russians?"

"More like their slaves."

"No longer. Stay where you are, and in the morning you may leave." He smiled suddenly. "We shall also be gone, of course. This castle, what is left of it, will not be safe for us now."

Krause let the tent flap open a bit more. "Who are you?" he asked.

The man bowed slightly. Now Krause could see his body as well as his terrifying face. He was dressed in black, in the fashion of a 16th Century nobleman, complete with sword. "I am Helmut, *Graf* von Grosshelm," he said. "I will not enter your tent, and you would be wise not to invite me in. It has been far too long since last I dined and I would not wish to harm my countrymen."

With that, the man turned on his heel and disappeared from sight.

The noise continued for another hour. Here and there came the sound of firing, mingled with the screams of the dying guards. The Germans remained in their tent, lying on the ground and hoping that no stray shot would find them. Krause had moved away from the door and was huddled with his men.

Eventually it grew silent in the compound, but still none of the Germans moved. Krause had told them what the ominous nobleman had said.

No one really believed him. If there was no firing now, it could as easily be presumed to mean that the Russians had triumphed.

Dawn came at last. Now the Germans began to hope. No one came to roust them out of their cots. No sound at all came from outside the tent. Only the soft whisper of the wind as it blew across the bare mountain top.

When they emerged the gates were wide open, and the compound was littered with the bodies of the Russian detachment. One of the braver men descended into the mountain, returning minutes later, his eyes wide with terror.

"They're all gone," he informed them. "The gate to the tomb is open, and all the coffins have been removed."

They would be, Krause thought. By now he knew what had happened, even if he couldn't quite bring himself to believe it. He was a modern man, not given to superstitious foolishness. Yet here it was before him. The Russian bodies all had their throats torn out, and there was no blood soaking into the ground around them.

It was the golden crucifix set on the short column directly in front of the tomb's gate, he thought. That had been the key, in a very literal sense. Someone had placed it there centuries before, knowing that the members of the ancient family entombed there were not really at rest. So long as the crucifix was in place they could not leave the tomb.

Then the Russian officer had taken it away. Krause didn't know how many vampires had been in the tomb. Enough, certainly. But the old *Graf* had somehow retained his sense of obligation to his own countrymen. The Russians were all dead, and the Germans were all alive.

And the vampires, after slaughtering the Russians, had taken up their coffins and moved to a safer place. If the Russians hadn't known what was in the tomb, it was certain that the locals did. Von Grosshelm and his un-dead clan would have wasted no time in relocating.

It was time, Krause decided, that his men did the same.

MISSION TWENTY-FIVE
[Writing as Jacob Thomson]

[This appeared on the jacobthomson.com web site as biographical material, supposedly telling the story of one of Thomson's wartime experiences in the Eighth Air Force during World War II. Since Thomson is really a pen name, and his biography just as fictional as his stories, it is here being properly presented as a short story.]

The view from the bombardier's position in the nose of a B-17 is fantastic. I first noticed this a few years ago, when someone brought a couple of old bombers to town and, for a price, took people for a ride. There was a B-17 and a B-24, both sitting there at the old airport. I'd never been up in a Liberator, and was naturally tempted to do so, but in the end nostalgia won out and I went up in the Flying Fortress instead.

How could I do otherwise? Not only was it the same type aircraft in which I'd flown over Germany during the war, but it was taking off from the same former Army airbase where I'd taken a lot of my training.

I naturally mentioned this to the guys operating the planes, and they let me fly in my old position. The view, as I said, was fantastic. Curiously, I'd never noticed it before, which I thought was a little odd, since I'd certainly seen some of the same things—though with a lot fewer houses and building—back in 1942. The airfield was well south of town in those days; now it's more or less in the middle of things, which is why they built a new one a few years ago.

I suppose it was the context. When I was first here, there was hardly time for sightseeing. We were learning to be bombardiers or gunners, not tourists. And once I was assigned to an active bomber flying out of England, well, most of what you'd see through the Plexiglas nose was either something you were trying to blow up, or something that was trying to kill you.

I'm sure there was some nice scenery to be seen flying over continental Europe, but the flak and enemy fighters tended to keep you a little preoccupied.

In the Eighth Air Force, the ultimate goal was 25 missions. If you made it that far you got to go home, where you would be put to work selling bonds, or training new aircrew. It doesn't seem like all that many at first. In theory, I suppose you could do all 25 missions within a couple of months. In practice, it took a lot longer. We didn't fly every day, after all. Sometimes you took off, but had to return without dropping your bombs because of engine trouble. All in all, it took us 16 months.

And that was the problem. The mission requirements and the loss rate tended to meet somewhere in the middle. The odds were against making it all the way. Some planes did. We did. Or, at least, seven of us did. And some of us didn't go home at all.

Our pilot called us "my crew." For the rest of us, we were "our crew," and that designation included the pilot. That was a difference. For the pilot it was "my" and for the rest of us "our." It was his plane, after all. It was his signature on the inventory card and, at least in theory, if he broke it they could make him pay for it.

Some of us stayed the same, others didn't. The pilot and co-pilot, the bombardier (me), our navigator, radio operator, flight engineer, and ball turret gunner, we all remained the same from the time the crew was formed and assigned to our plane. The two waist gunners and the tail gunner changed.

Our original tail gunner was replaced after the 12th mission, and we lost our right waist gunner on mission 18. *His* replacement was killed on the next mission, before we really had a chance to get to know him. Our left waist gunner was with us until Mission 23, and his loss hit everyone particularly hard, not only because by then there were only two more missions to go, but also because we didn't know his fate.

Our original tail and right waist gunners had been wounded, bad enough for a ticket home, but not bad enough that they would be seriously inconvenienced later in life. We missed them, naturally, but we knew they'd be okay in the long run.

The first replacement right waist gunner was missed, but not as much. As I said, we just didn't know him that long. He was a member of our crew for less than a week.

But when our left waist gunner was hit by a shell from a FW-190, it wasn't a minor wound. The explosive shell nearly took off his left leg. About all we could do for him was tie a tourniquet around his leg above the gaping wound, put him in his parachute, and shove him out of the plane over Wilhelmshaven. The last we saw of him was as his parachute opened. There were still fighters around, as well as flak, and no one had time to watch him as he descended. We weren't really worried about someone shooting him in his parachute on the way down. That didn't happen nearly as often as some stories would have you think, and most of the time it probably wasn't deliberate—just a case of winding up in the middle of a battle and catching a stray bullet. All we could do was hope the Germans would find him quickly and get him to a hospital.

As it turned out, they did. We didn't find out until about a month later, when word made it back through the Swiss Red Cross. He lost the leg, but he survived the war. The last I heard he was still living in Chicago.

Our final mission was supposed to be a milk run. No one believed it. Once we found out where we were going, we recognized that it would be easier to fly to St. Nazaire, drop our bombs on the U-Boat pens there, and make a quick run back across Biscay than to fly a mission to Berlin, but planes were lost on short missions, too. It wasn't how far you had to fly, after all, so much as how good the enemy fighter pilots happened to be that day, how accurate their flak gunners might be, and, even more, if you were lucky. You could as easily die from an accident as from enemy action.

As we prepared for our 23rd mission, the one where we lost our left waist gunner, another plane, situated halfway across the field, simply vanished as her entire bomb load went up at once. She took five other planes with her, though fortunately the other planes were lost from blast damage from the first plane and their own bombs didn't go up. More men were killed in that accident than on the actual raid.

Now, as we prepared for the final mission we would fly as a crew before returning to the States, it was hard for me not think of that explosion. It came with my job. I was squatting on the narrow catwalk inside the bomb bay, installing the fuses with the help of a tech sergeant armorer, which was precisely what had been going on when the other bomber blew up. It was a touchy job. The bombs were pretty much just big chunks of inert metal, despite being stuffed with high explosive, until the fuses were inserted and tightened. One went in the nose, another in the tail. Redundancy meant there was a second chance; if one fuse failed to function on impact, the other could still set off the bomb. In this case, the nose fuse was set to detonate nearly instantaneously, a tenth of a second after impact. The tail fuse had a 45 second delay.

The arming job went on in silence, both of us concentrating very hard on what we were doing. The rest of the ground crew was keeping a respectful distance. If the plane blew up they'd still all go with it, but there's some psychological reassurance in standing back and watching from a distance and, in any case, for the most part their jobs were done until the plane returned. As for me, I didn't worry about it that much. I hadn't managed to blow up anything except a target so far and, when you considered it, the odds were pretty good that I wouldn't do it this day, either.

Once the bombs were armed, the sergeant departed and the bomb bay doors were closed. I went forward, taking my place in the nose. It was going to be an uncomfortable ride, as it always was. In retrospect, it's perhaps a bit surprising how little thought Boeing had given to crew safety during flight. Not protection from the enemy, but protection from the plane itself. Only the captain and co-pilot had seat belts and shoulder harnesses. For everyone else it was just hang on as best you can. On my recent jaunt, all of the passengers were properly strapped into seats for takeoff and landing, allowed to move about the plane only after she reached her cruising altitude. In combat, you flew at your position and just held on.

Once all the pre-flight checks were satisfactorily completed, we settled in to wait. Some days that wait lasted an eternity, and was followed by the anti-climax of a canceled mission. Today it lasted only half an hour before the signal to start engines was given.

One by one, the four big Wright engines turned over and roared to life. This was the point where we might be given a reprieve. It had happened before, five times, when an engine had either refused to start, or wouldn't run properly. Those times we had stayed behind while the mechanics went to work on the engine. But this time they all ran smoothly, and after another brief wait our plane began to move.

I was always relieved once the takeoff run was completed and we were actually in the air. Runways are never more than a transitional area, and airplanes belong in the air, not bouncing along the ground at an ever-increasing speed as they try to get there. With the wheels up the ride smoothed out, though it would never be as smooth as a commercial airliner. Even if the air is perfectly smooth, a couple hundred big four-engined bombers flying in formation create more than enough turbulence.

The Forts, at least, were good fliers.

We joined up and the formation headed for the target. Since we were only going as far as the French coast, it would be a relatively short mission, most of it over water. Flying over water had both good and bad aspects. The good part was that flak would be limited to the time actually over the target, as there was no really practical way to position the guns in the sea. The bad part was that, if you went down, your chances of surviving were much worse than over land, where you at least wouldn't have to worry about drowning.

We crossed the English coast at 0837. Flying time to the target from that point should be 49 minutes. During the majority of the flight, the pilot would fly the plane. That was what the Army paid him to do. But the final few minutes as we made the run in to the target the plane would be on auto pilot, which was under my control, not the pilot's. The actual bomb run was always the worst part. In order to get the bombs on target, the plane had to fly straight and level on a precise course over the target.

Now, when I say over the target, I don't mean the plane would have to fly directly over the target. The bombs were dropped well before we crossed over the target, momentum carrying them forward in a curving path toward the earth. Once they were gone, the plane's course would have no further effect on their trajectory and we could start dodging. Until they were gone, it didn't matter what the enemy threw at us, be it clouds of flak or swarms of fighters, for we could not alter course even slightly if we expected our bombs to hit.

The story was that our Norden bombsight was so accurate that it could drop a bomb into a pickle barrel from 20,000 feet. I never came close to that sort of accuracy, and I doubt anyone else did, either. Hitting something that small from that high didn't really become practical until laser guided bombs came along years later. I figured I could put our load into a football field, though, which was good enough for the time. We didn't rely on real precision. We just dumped several tons of bombs in as tight a pattern as possible and hoped for the best.

Our flight path took us southwest initially, staying well offshore as we rounded the French coast. The idea was to stay out of range of artillery and, with luck, avoid notice by German fighter forces until we turned east and ran in to the target from the Bay of Biscay. The shortest route would have been almost due south, but that required flying over France and gave the enemy a lot more time to cause a fuss. The Germans had fairly effective air warning radar by then, and a flight of 60 B-17s makes a pretty big target.

A direct route would also have taken us over other strongly defended targets. If we had no intention of bombing Brest, there was no point in risking the planes by flying through its defenses.

The sky was clear as we turned east for the run in to the target. There would be no place to hide on this trip. Ceiling and visibility were both unlimited, making conditions ideal for accurate bombing. Unfortunately, it also meant conditions were ideal for the German fighters and flak gunners.

To be honest, my idea of perfect conditions were thick clouds with an opening directly above the target just large enough to make the bomb run.

Ten minutes later the French coast was in sight. The formation made a minor course correction, and I prepared to take over for the bomb run. Two minutes out the pilot handed off control. This was the hard part. The plane would have to fly dead steady for the next two or three minutes or the bombs would miss.

By now, the Germans had noticed we were there. The clear sky ahead blossomed with hundreds of red flashes, instantly resolving themselves into cottony puffs of smoke. They looked harmless enough from a distance, but the clouds of smoke were filled with shards of jagged steel that could rip a plane to pieces. It wasn't even necessary for the flak shell to explode close to the plane. Simply flying through the falling shell fragments could take out an engine or rip through the cockpit and kill the flight crew.

We had done these missions before, so it was hard not to wonder if we were really accomplishing anything. The primary targets were the U-boat pens, and each plane carried a full bomb load, six big thousand-pound bombs. But the U-boat pen roofs were solid, reinforced concrete, 23 feet thick. A thousand-pound bomb would hardly make a dent in that. Our only hope, really, was to drop as many bombs as possible in the same spot and hope the combined detonations would be enough to bring down the roof.

So far, they hadn't been. The British were working on special bombs, and we had some hope they would work. As for our efforts, you had to wonder if we were being much more than a nuisance. Unless we happened to catch a U-boat in the open there wasn't that much we could do to destroy it.

The plane was jumping now, as the flak bursts drew closer. The German gunners clearly had our altitude and there wasn't a damned thing we could do about it until the bombs were dropped.

The nose compartment was suddenly bathed in a dappled glow as a bursting shell shredded the skin on the port side. I felt something grab at my thick jacket. But I was lucky. The shell fragment had torn a long rip in the heavy leather as it shot across my back, but hadn't penetrated.

I bent over the bombsight again, watching as the target crawled into the crosshairs. Only a few more seconds now. Then, "Bombs away!"

The plane jumped upward as 6,000 pounds of ordnance dropped from the bomb bay and started down toward the U-boat pen.

"Pilot's plane," came over the intercom.

It took just over a minute for all of the planes to drop their bombs. After that, the formation turned northwest, heading back out to sea. As we emerged from the cloud of flak, the fighters roared in. Every gun in the formation opened up at once.

Our bombs gone, I grabbed the nose-mounted .50-caliber machine-gun and swung it toward an oncoming Messerschmidt. That was a favorite tactic of the German fighters, to come in from dead ahead, where our armament was weakest and the guns were manned by the bombardier and navigator, who might well be preoccupied with other things. It was a weakness that would be fixed with the addition of a remote controlled chin turret mounting a pair of .50-caliber machine-guns.

We didn't have the chin turret, so our ability to respond to an oncoming enemy was considerably less than with later models. The machine-gun bucked in my hands as I opened fire. In this situation it was really a question of who would flinch first, or who would kill the other.

The German fighter dove under our nose. I did my best to put a burst into his engine or cockpit, but I could see the tracers missing to one side. A few rounds certainly went into his wing, but there was no way to tell if I'd done any real damage.

For the next quarter hour the fighters chased our formation away from the coast. The crew kept up a constant chatter, one report following another, as they fired at the pursuing Messerschmidts and Focke-Wulfs. There were only two things that mattered now. One was keeping the enemy fighters at bay, and the other was staying with the formation. As heavily armed as a B-17 might be, it was still a big, relatively slow target for a fighter once separated from the supporting fire of the formation.

No more fighters attacked from ahead, but the navigator and I kept up our vigilance. It only took one fighter slipping in at the wrong time and we'd be dead. Now, with the bombs gone and the planes on the way home, the risk seemed that much greater. Many raids had lost more planes on the way back from the target, so there was never a time when you could really relax. That would have to wait until the plane had landed.

And then we were in the clear. The fighters had turned back, and the bombers lumbered on, our formation still mostly intact. Sixty planes had started out on the raid, and fifty-four were coming back. I still wasn't ready to declare us safe, though. We would be within range of German fighters for at least the next half hour. Our immediate pursuers had gone, probably low on fuel, but that didn't mean they couldn't send fresh planes after us.

For that matter, there was nothing to stop the Germans from sending out fresh fighters as we approached the English coastline. We would be back in range of German air bases in northern France at that time. And, if not fighters, they could send a bombing raid against the airfields as we came in to land.

We were sweating all the way back. I was, at least. And I don't suppose anyone else felt any more complacent. If we made it back, we'd get to go home. But we hadn't made it yet.

Finally, a little more than three hours after taking off, our pilot eased the plane down onto the runway. Even then I wasn't quite ready to relax. Knowing we had survived, there was still a sense of unease. The enemy bombers could still come in the night. Something could happen on the way home. And, of course, after we finished our rotation back to training duty in the States, there was always the chance they'd send us right back here.

But, for the moment, the greatest risk was behind us. We had survived, most of us, and it was time to go home, sell war bonds, and hope for the best.

RETURN TO DUTY

[This is another Gehunite Empire story, set during the same period as *Element of Surprise.* This story consists of parts of chapters one and two of my 1981 novel, *The Highest Honour,* most of which has been lost.]

The battered old Oshroreno saloon lurched drunkenly on its worn suspension as the Marine driver swerved to avoid a deep hole in the ill-maintained road. It did him little good, for a moment later the left front wheel found an even more impressive crater to explore, and did so with an enthusiastic 'Crack!' as the seals in the much abused shock absorber blew out.

In the back seat, Commander Julia Maniah gritted her teeth and peered resignedly out the window into the darkness. It was claimed that even in peacetime the government could find plenty of places to waste money. Obviously repairing the roads inside the sprawling Koril Harbour Naval Base, which surrounded the entire southern branch of Tufaria Bay, wasn't one of them.

"This car," the Marine grunted, "could use some work." The broken shock was now banging and bouncing at the slightest bump, and he was visible straining to control the vehicle.

"Yes," Maniah said. Repair these roads, she thought, and buy a few new staff cars. Those would be *my* priorities if I could run the world for a month or two!

They were just past the big Naval Hospital now, and into the dependent housing area, where the roads were, if anything, even worse. The potholed roads were a stark contrast to the orderly rows of neat houses, each with its carefully manicured front garden and, white painted wood fences. It was still quite dark, with here and there a light visible in the gloom as evidence that at least a few others were going to be pulling duty this New Year's Holiday morning.

Then the darkness erupted into a fierce ball of flame and noise about a hundred metres in front of the slow-moving staff car, which seemed to leap clear of the cratered road at the concussion. A few fragments of burning wood fell around and onto the car as the driver stood on the brakes. Then they were both out of the car and running toward the furiously burning house.

"What the hell was that?" the Marine shouted. He had stopped about 20 metres from the blazing house, the heat intense even at that distance.

Maniah was standing beside him, shielding her face with her left arm. The heat, she noticed, was quickly diminishing, the billowing flames subsiding to gnaw at the wooden house. "Hydrogen explosion," she said. "Most likely."

"It's the back of the house that blew out," the Marine said, nodding. "Yes, I'm sure you're right, ma'am." He pointed to where most of one wall had been blown out. "That would have been the kitchen there. A hydrogen supply line must have started to leak during the night and filled the kitchen, and when someone went to light the stove…"

Maniah nodded. It might not have even been somebody. All it would take was a spark. An automatic coffee maker switching on, a faulty refrigerator motor. Under the right circumstances, even someone touching a metal door knob.

She felt a sudden chill as a terrified, inhuman scream pierced through the crackling of burning wood. Stabbing right to the soul. It had come from inside the blazing house. Someone was still alive in there.

"Get the crash axe from the car!" she snapped.

The Marine, who had been standing as if turned to stone since that first horrible shriek, responded automatically to the tone of command. Without a word he was running back toward the car.

Maniah hurried around to the other side of the house. The wind carried the stink of burning wood and upholstery—and worse—to her nostrils, and it was all she could do to keep from vomiting. She has smelt burning flesh once before, and the stench brought back the still too-vivid memory of escaping from the blazing fourth floor of her dormitory at the Imperial Naval College near the end of her second year. One hundred nineteen second year cadets had been killed in that fire, including her own roommate.

From inside the house there came another scream. A scream of pure terror, much as she had heard when one of the cadets had dived from the dormitory roof, her hair and clothing burning like a torch as she fell.

Maniah nearly tripped over a small sign on the lawn. *Regimental Sergeant Major Ehon Onimwe, Imperial Marines*, it said. She wondered if it was the sergeant major who was screaming like that.

Her driver came pounding up, the axe carried diagonally across his body, like a rifle at high port. He looked calmer now, his training kicking in, duty pushing any fear out of the way. "Now what, ma'am?"

"Give me the axe," she said. "Then see if that hosepipe still works."

"Yes, ma'am!" The Marine uncoiled the hose from its bracket on the side of the house and twisted the cock. Inside the wall the piping shuddered and banged, but then water was pouring from the brass nozzle in a hard stream.

Maniah smashed out a window with the axe, raking the blade around the frame to knock out the jagged shards. "Follow me with that hose," she snapped, climbing through the window and into the house.

She was in a bedroom, and here the air was quite free of smoke. Again she heard the screaming, coming from somewhere deeper in the house, beyond the closed door. Somehow she remembered to feel the door before trying to open it. It was warm, but not hot, but still she hesitated, knowing that if there was fire beyond the door opening it might admit enough oxygen to cause a flashback.

"Put some water on that door," she ordered.

The Marine did as he was told. After a moment, Maniah reached out and turned the brass handle. The door opened slowly, revealing a central hall, with smoke hanging in a thick cloud just at head height, and flames creeping along the ceiling and upper walls.

Bending low to keep below the thick smoke, Maniah plunged into the hall, with the hose-wielding Marine at her heels. At the far end a door stood against the wall, only the bottom hinge retaining a precarious hold, keeping it from crashing into the burning kitchen beyond. The shattered iron hulk of the stove lay across a charred, burning *thing* that might once have been human. Beyond it a long jet of flame rose from the broken hydrogen supply line.

Again she heard the screaming, and now she was close enough to find the source. Another door, close to the shattered kitchen, and on the far side of the hall from where they had entered.

Something warm brushed her neck, and a moment later she could feel the hose being sprayed over her. The bloody ceiling was going to collapse on top of them if they didn't get out of there damned quick, she realised. And at that moment, they were without even the dubious protection of a fire-fighter's helmet and rubberised canvas turnout coat.

The door was locked. *Naturally.* Just as naturally, there was no key in the lock. Muttering imprecations, she smashed the axe into the flimsy lock four times before it gave way and the door swung open.

It was another bedroom. The ceiling was alight, probably from above, she thought, the fire working its way through the attic. The glow provided enough light for her to find the screaming child, huddled in a corner, behind a tall dresser. He looked to be no more than four or five.

Dropping the axe, Maniah scooped up the child. The Marine was opening the window. It would be foolish to go back through the burning house with a direct exit available. He went out first, taking the child from her as soon as he was outside, then helping her down from the window. They were hardly out when part of the bedroom ceiling collapsed.

The base fire brigade was just pulling up in front of the house as they emerged. The child was turned over to a white-coated sick berth attendant, and Maniah sank down gratefully onto the damp grass alongside the pumper truck. One of the fire-fighters clapped a respirator mask over her face, and close by she saw the Marine getting the same treatment

The SBA had another mask on the little boy, and after a few minutes he nodded and smiled. So at least we didn't risk our necks for nothing, Maniah thought. So long as the boy was healthy, it had been worth the risk.

As Maniah related her story to the fire brigade captain—his actual rank was chief petty officer—a new Ahonnoro saloon pulled up to the kerb and disgorged a worried-looking man in Marine battle dress, with the triple chevrons and bars of a regimental sergeant major on his shoulder straps.

The boy's father?

A moment later the boy confirmed her guess. Evidently more terrified than hurt by his ordeal, the boy pulled away from the SBA, ran to the newcomer, and leapt into his arms.

They were both crying quite unashamedly.

Maniah thought suddenly of the charred corpse in the blasted kitchen. The boy's mother, almost certainly. There would be more to cry about than simple relief.

* * *

The first hint of false dawn was just tinting the eastern sky as the battered old staff car resumed its interrupted journey. The five minute drive to the main gate of the Submarine Base was completed in silence, driver and passenger both too drained to know quite what to say.

Then the car had pulled up at the gate, and the Marine driver was opening the door for his passenger and going around to collect her single small bag from the boot. He placed it by her feet and saluted. The normally perfect salute of an Imperial Marine seemed somehow even more perfect in the faint light of dawn

"Thank you, Corporal," Maniah said, returning the salute. "You did a fine job back there. I want you to know that."

"You did pretty good yourself, ma'am," he replied. "For a sailor."

The commander laughed. "We all have our little faults," she said, picking up her bag. They were grinning like conspirators.

Finally, the Marine returned to the car and drove away. He would have an interesting story to tell him wife when he got home, Maniah thought. He would also have some appropriate medal. She would see to that.

The guard in the little shack by the gate was looking at her curiously. He was a Marine sergeant, very smartly turned out, wearing a military police brassard on his left sleeve and a large pistol in a gleaming leather holster on his right hip.

Maniah couldn't see her face, but her white trousers were covered with soot, there was a big grass stain on the seat, and her hair was scorched in back where something burning had fallen on her. She had to be a mess, she thought, as she approached the gate.

Above it, a weathered sign advised and warned.

SUBMARINE BASE, KORIL HARBOUR
AUTHORISED PERSONNEL ONLY

When she came into the light by the guard shack, the guard looked at her even more closely. News of what had happened in the housing area had yet to spread, so all he knew was that he was being confronted with a very filthy naval officer. He did not appear to approve.

"Identity card, please, Commander."

Maniah handed it over. The guard studied it dubiously, carefully comparing the picture with the woman standing in front of him. Finally, after what seemed an eternity, he handed it back and saluted.

"Welcome back, ma'am," he said. He sounded as if he were lying.

"Thank you." Maniah just sounded tired. The fire had taken more out of her than she had thought.

All I want to do, she decided, is get into a shower, and then into my bunk, and stay there until it gets dark again. There wasn't the slightest possibility of that happening, she was sure. No doubt she could manage the shower and a clean uniform, but there was too much work to do, with her boat getting ready to leave dock tomorrow.

Her heels clicked dispiritedly on the unbroken pavement inside the submarine base. There was less traffic here, and the base was commanded by a crusty old rear admiral who was quite happy to put some of her trainees to work repairing roads if the government couldn't get the job done.

Looking down the road, past the headquarters building on the point, she could see the sky growing perceptibly brighter. Very soon now the sun would be rising over the broad anchorage, with the dozens of warship anchored there showing first their silhouettes, and then their details as the sun rose higher into the eastern sky.

Already people were up and moving about, holiday or no. A squad of enlisted trainees passed her at the double, goaded along by an iron-lunged petty officer. They would hate this daily morning run, Maniah was certain of that. Only the real keep fit fanatics enjoyed it. Later, though, after they were sent to the fleet, assigned to their first boat, they might look back with a certain touch of nostalgia on a time when running was possible. When any meaningful exercise was possible.

Most of the trainees would begin their careers in one of the older boats, with their light oil burning compression-ignition engines[1] for surface run-

---

1   Diesels, essentially, but as these people lived roughly 85,000 years before Rudolf Diesel was born, they named the engines after the way they worked and not after a German engineer who would discover the same system millennia

ning, and massive banks of battery cells to power the motors when submerged. Only the two or three best out of each cycle would go straight to nuclear power school. The rest would have to earn their way onto the new boats by being outstanding in the old ones.

She smiled suddenly, remembering her own time in those old boats. How pleasant it had been to surface in calm weather, and jump around on the upper deck. Or the unpleasant times, the horrible feeling that you were going to burst open when running submerged on the engines and a wave closed the intake valve in the snorkel, causing the engines to suck all the air out of the pressure hull before the valve opened again.

Still, at least those old boats *had* a deck, and when they were surfaced you could make use of it. The old boats were *called* submarines, but they were really surface ship that were capable of submerging for a limited time.

The nuclear boats usually submerged as soon as they were past the sea frontier and didn't surface again until they returned to base. There was nothing that could really be called a deck on any of them now. Line handlers were issued special deck shoes that could get a grip on the curved upper hull casing. The hulls had a characteristic teardrop shape for efficiency while submerged, and the conning tower superstructure of the old boats had been replaced by a slender fin, with a tiny cockpit at the top, and a small, glazed wheelhouse just below it where the helmsman could steer when the boat was surfaced.

Being able to see was useful when manoeuvring in a crowded harbour, or when approaching a dock.

Maniah walked between the Maintenance Shed and the Special Equipment Warehouse and out onto the lip of the dock. Below her, sitting on keel blocks in a dried out basin that had originally been built to accommodate long vanished wooden first rates, was her own command.

His Imperial Majesty's Submarine *Warrior*.

A long, streamlined black teardrop for a hull, with the slender fin rising about one third of the way back, and a streamlined hump on the bow that held part of the detection gear. At the stern were rudders and diving planes, just in front of the big, seven-bladed bronze screw, with its hollow shaft for deploying the towed array listening gear that had eliminated the old blind spot right aft.

Ugly as sin, Maniah thought. Like a beached whale.

Ugly, and when you thought about it, perhaps even a traitor of sorts within its underwater family. For *Warrior* had been designed and built, right from the first, for the primary purpose of hunting down and killing other submarines. She was a final refinement of the earlier 'killer' submarines, which had resulted from some admirals' finally grasping the obvious. The best way to hunt down and destroy a submarine was with another submarine.

Surface escorts were limited in their ability to track and attack sub-

later.

marines. For one thing, because of the turbulence created as the escort passed through the water, surface sonar was nearly useless at speeds much in excess of 22 knots. That wasn't much of problem back in the days when few subs could manage more than 9 knots submerged, but a definite handicap once nuclear boats entered the picture.

Submarines didn't have that problem. Once you were deep enough, the turbulence problem ceased. Water pressure was great enough to eliminate cavitation. On the surface, most of the power was wasted creating a bow wave. Deep beneath the surface, the water parted smoothly around the hull and came back together at the stern.

Now that improvements in sonar and computers allowed accurate attacks from as deep as 200 metres, submarines had really come into their own as the premier anti-submarine platform. In a properly conducted attack, an enemy wouldn't know he was being tracked until the hunter had fired.

Strangely, the only time *Warrior* had ever used her awesome capabilities to the full in hunting another sub had been a year ago, when *Terrible*, an elderly nuclear attack boat, had been reported overdue from a routine patrol. *Warrior* had located some wreckage, scattered over the seabed at 2,800 metres. Far below safe diving depth for any submarine.

The Navy had borrowed a special research sub from the Cartographic Institute, which in addition to mapping the continents and islands, was also charged with charting everything under the seas. The research sub was capable of diving a good bit deeper than the wreckage, and had a mechanical arm and "hand" for collecting things from the ocean floor. It had brought up a length of piping with *Terrible*'s number etched on it, confirming that the old boat had somehow dropped too deep and imploded from the sea pressure.

Other than the waiting, knowing what was coming, Maniah suspected it wasn't that bad a way to go. You didn't drown at those depths. When the hull imploded the air pressure inside the sub spiked, the temperature rose instantly to well over 1,000 degrees, and anyone inside the boat was vaporised. You were simply alive one instant and the next instant you were not. It sound awful in the abstract, but the reality was instant oblivion.

She shook her head. Why was she thinking about this now? The fire, she supposed. She really should get back to her quarters and change out of her filthy, smoke-stained uniform.

Instead, she walked out to the end of the dock, past the unmanned anti-aircraft guns zipped up in their canvas covers. In the early morning light, the vast Koril Harbour naval anchorage looked particularly impressive, with so much of the fleet in harbour for the New Years Holiday. Impressive, she thought, but also deceptive. This year, the 382nd of the Empire, was starting out by fooling anyone who looked at the vast collection of ships.

Just across the anchorage, at the destroyer base, an even dozen of the swift killers were rafted alongside the big tender, *Omani River*. They looked restless, eager to return to sea and the chase. But Maniah knew perfectly well that only two of them could have managed to get under way in anything less than a fortnight. The rest were sealed up for long term storage, just in case they were ever needed again.

In the southwest anchorage, four huge fleet carriers swung regally at their buoys. From the deck of the closest a bugle was sounding Sunrise. The carriers, at least, were components of the active fleet. Or three of them were. The fourth, the largest, *Emperor Felim*, was due to enter dock in a few days for an extensive refit and renewal of her reactor cores.

Further up the anchorage, the piled-up grey bulks of the old battleships and cruisers were silhouetted against the rising sun. Their day was past, Maniah thought, with their big guns rendered impotent by carrier aircraft. The big ships didn't dare go anywhere without their own air cover, so now they were tied to the carriers for safety, and retained mostly for shore bombardment. That was the one thing a battleship could still do better than any aeroplane.

There was a sudden bright flash near the mouth of the bay, and a few seconds later the boom of a distant explosion rolled over the water. What the hell? Another accident? There was nothing on that point but a radar station, a small anti-aircraft battery, and a Coastal Patrol lifesaving station. Had someone been so stupid as to smoke in the ammo bunker?

Remembering the glasses in their pressure-tight container on the bridge, Maniah hurried back along the dock and across the brow. It seemed to take forever to climb the fin, but at least the glasses were still there. It wouldn't have surprised her to find they'd gone home with some anonymous dockyard worker.

There was another flash on the point as she was lifting the glasses to her eyes, and as she spun the focus wheel she could hear the delayed boom of the explosion. And there was another sound now, more ominous than any explosion. Aero engines. A lot of them, and coming closer.

The sound was a frightening mix of jets and propeller driven planes. As she looked, they started to come into view. Sleek jet fighters, escorting big, single engine prop jobs. Those frightened her more than the jets. The last time she had seen planes like these was at the airport in Talim. Devastator torpedo bombers, with the blue and gold flag of Arzucalda vivid on wings and tail, and a single torpedo hanging beneath each of them.

It was only as the leading plane roared past that the first sirens began to scream their warning. Someone had been caught napping, she thought, and now it was too late.

Someone emerged through the hatch by her feet, but her concentration on the attacking torpedo bombers was too intense for her to notice who it was. At the moment, that just didn't seem important.

Now the leading Devastator was streaking low across the choppy water toward the anchored carriers. As she watched, the slim torpedo dropped from its shackles and plunged into the harbour, while the plane roared up and over the carrier, the wing mounted cannon spitting fire, the curving arcs of orange tracer ripping into the scrambling crew, cutting them down like wheat before the reaper as they broke from their orderly morning formations and ran, half-panicked, to their action stations. Across the water came the screams of the wounded, mingling horribly with the clamour of alarm bells and sirens, and the crash of exploding bombs, chattering machine-guns, and cannon, and the roar of screaming aero engines as the first wave of torpedo bombers released their loads and hurried away.

A tall column of brown and white water reared up alongside the nearest carrier as the first torpedo smashed home. Two more exploded within seconds of the first, seeming to lift the massive hull from the water. Almost at once the stricken vessel began to heel over alarmingly to port, her hull fatally holed in three places.

"The murdering bastards!"

For the first time Maniah fully realised that she was not alone on the bridge. The first lieutenant, Rae Ahno, was standing beside her, his eyes locked on the sinking carrier and the hapless sailors who were dropping from the tilting deck into the filthy water. Swimming for their lives, fearful of being dragged down by the suction from the sinking ship.

Not much worry about that, she thought. At low tide there was only about ten metres of water under the carrier. Most of the ship would still be out of the water, even sitting on the bottom.

"How many of our crew are aboard, Rae?" Maniah asked.

Ahno looked at her blankly. It seemed that she had not been the only one too preoccupied to notice someone on the tiny bridge.

"What?"

"I asked, how many are aboard?"

"Oh." He shook his head. "Just the duty part of the watch. Defaulters, mostly. And 'essential' personnel.' The rest aren't due back until Sunset."

An Arzucaldan dive bomber plummeted toward them, and the two officers dropped hurriedly below the level of the curved screen. The bomb detached itself as the plane pulled out of its near vertical dive, seeming to plunge right at them until, at the last moment, it became clear that it was not going to hit them.

There was a tremendous blast from the adjacent dock. A jagged fragment of hull plating clattered off the top of the fin and fell into the bridge, where it lay vibrating on the grating.

"Close," Ahno muttered.

"Too close," Maniah said. "Get everyone out of the boat right now. We make too good a target just sitting in dock like this."

"Aye, aye, ma'am."

"And send some of them to man that anti-aircraft gun at the end of the dock if no one else turns up to do it."

"Right." Ahno bent over the bridge intercom and pressed the TALK button. "Attention! Attention! Clear the boat! All hands clear the boat at once!

Armourer, muster a party on the dock to man the anti-aircraft battery!"

He released the switch and straightened up. "That should get them moving," he said. Now that the first shock had passed he felt quite calm, detached from the mounting horror, and ready to handle whatever the rest of this deadly holiday might demand.

Maniah nodded. It seemed almost too much to absorb at once. First the fire. That had been bad enough. Taken too much from her. Brought back those memories of the Naval College fire all those years ago, of the friends lost to an unfeeling, incorporeal enemy.

And now this. Was there room enough left in the day for another disaster? She pulled back her cuff and glanced at the display on her watch. Only 0919. There was still plenty of time left to die.

"Let's get down onto the dock," she said at last.

Ahno nodded and dropped down the hatch. He obviously had no intention of climbing down the outside of the fin while there were enemy fighters streaking around overhead looking for targets. Directly he had dropped out of sight she followed, pulling the hatch shut behind her.

They had just emerged through the screen door at the base of the fin when a tremendous column of smoke and fire rose to the southeast, a furiously climbing pillar of flame and smoke and debris that was now beginning to spread outward at the top, like a giant mushroom, as the sound of the monstrous detonation reached the dock area.

"The Fleet Air Base," Ahno whispered. "It has to be. Nothing else there." He looked at her nervously. "The bastards must have made a direct hit on the bomb storage."

Maniah returned his glance and nodded gravely, the sudden concern clear on her smudged face. Her younger brother was a seniorlieutenant in the Fleet Air Arm, stationed at the Koril Harbour Fleet Air Base, flying his Demon fighter every chance he could get.

"I just hope the fighters made it into the air before the enemy could get to them," she said. "If the planes were destroyed on the ground, there's nothing much left to defend this place."

Ahno shuddered. "Don't even consider it."

"I have to." She managed a weak smile. "Comes with the job."

On the dock, the crew had formed up briefly. The armourer had selected eight of them, all but one born troublemakers, if their service records were any indication, and harried them down to the still shrouded anti-aircraft gun as the end of the dock. Troublemakers or not, Maniah thought, they were the most experienced personnel aboard this morning.

The other nine ratings stood around in a tight little knot, unsure of what to do next. They were, she noticed, the greenest of the crew, most of them barely out of submarine school. Four of them hadn't even begun the work of qualifying in submarines and earning the gold badge that would mark them apart from the mass of surface sailors.

The one exception was the tall, broken-nosed Callaaite petty officer

Sick Berth Attendant, who had come up from his duty station carrying the portable medical kit. The man was experienced enough to stand in for a qualified physician, should it become necessary. But even he looked utterly confused by this sudden turn of events.

No one was expecting a war, Maniah thought. A half smiled formed momentarily. Least of all me!

*   *   *

Chief Petty Officer Armourer Kalor Ulanik emerged from the gun tub, his strong, lined face set in an expression of barely contained fury. The gun was in perfect condition, and it was absolutely bloody useless! There wasn't a single round of 5 CM ammunition to be found anywhere on the dock. And the telephone was ruined. Smashed to fragments by a jagged scrap of casing blasted from *Harrier*, the boat in the adjacent dock.

A pretty, young ordinary sailor followed him from the gun tub, her oversized helmet bobbing with every step. "What do we do now, Chief?" she asked.

He rounded on her, his pale brown eyes blazing. "Who the hell told you to leave your..." With a visible effort he managed to get his temper back under control. It wasn't this infant's fault that some idiot had failed to provide ammunition for the gun. "Sorry," he grunted. "Go tell the captain there's no ammo here. Tell her I need as much 5 CM, type 3 ammo as she can lay hands on. Got that, Vonda?"

"Five CM, type 3 ammunition. Got it, Chief."

"Right. Get moving."

Give me patience, Ulanik thought, as the young sailor hurried off to find the captain. She'd just joined, after all, only a week out of school and never nearer fighting that a target range. He shook his head. *I* was like that once, L'Mik help me.

Commander Maniah came trotting up, young Vonda at her heels.

"Isn't there anything you can do, Armourer?" Maniah asked.

"Not with empty guns, ma'am," Ulanik replied. "I guess the powers that be weren't expecting the Arzucaldans to start something just now.

Who was? She said, "The first lieutenant is trying to get through to headquarters now. If there's any ammunition to be had, he'll get it for you. Eventually." She looked disgusted. "Between the attack and the holiday today everything is completely fucked up. No one seems to know where anyone else is—or even who's supposed to be there in the first place."

The ginger haired chief petty officer nodded resignedly. "That's the Service for you, ma'am. Takes a war to wake everyone up, and unless *we* start the bloody thing they'll still sleep through the first week."

None of them heard the explosion. There was simply a tremendous pressure, flinging them roughly to the asphalt surface of the dock. Maniah felt something heavy falling roughly across her legs, pinning them. Her left elbow stung viciously where the rough paving had scraped away the heavy cloth of her uniform jacket and shirt sleeve, taking a thin layer of hide with them. Her ears were ringing viciously, and her head felt only loosely attached.

It was some moments before she realised what had actually happened.

When she again looked out over the anchorage the *Emperor Almak*, a giant fleet carrier less than five years old, was gone. There was only a circle of foaming water, and a huge pillar of smoke. A bomb must have penetrated a magazine, she thought. Nothing else could have done that, destroyed the giant ship so utterly in a few terrible seconds.

Ulanik picked himself up off the captain's legs, muttering an apology that died on his tongue as he stared in sudden shock at the dock a few feet beyond her.

Maniah followed his eyes and nearly gagged. Ordinary Sailor Alla Vonda was lying face up on the asphalt, her eyes wide open and staring blankly at the sky, a jagged shard of plating protruding from the middle of her forehead.

There was surprisingly little blood on the dead sailor's face, and she looked more surprised than anything else, with her eyes bulging slightly from the impact.

SeniorLieutenant Rae Ahno came up the brow from *Warrior*, hurrying to join them. He spared the dead sailor only a brief, uninterested glance before getting down to business. Maniah wondered if he was really so deadly calm? Or was he just in shock and somehow functioning despite that?

"I finally got through to someone at headquarters," he said. "It seems that the ammunition is kept locked up at the central armoury to prevent it being stolen from the gun emplacements." He shrugged resignedly. "Though I can't think of what anyone would do with one of those shells once he had it."

"Make an interesting paperweight," Ulanik commented, "if you were careful."

The first lieutenant laughed, a short, harsh bark that served only to reveal just how tightly his nerves were stretched. "Perhaps," he said. "In any case, the woman assured me that ammunition will be forthcoming. After they've supplied all the guns protecting the battleship and cruiser anchorage, that is."

"Bloody wonderful!" Ulanik muttered. "Those great bastards can protect *themselves*. They've been firing since this mess started! They don't have to get ammo from shore storage, they carry their own."

He stared out over the anchorage to where the big capital ships rode at their buoys, their sides rippling with flame as their anti-aircraft and secondary batteries kept up a steady fire on the attacking planes. "What the hell do they expect us to do until we're supplied," Ulanik complained, "fire a torpedo at an aeroplane?"

Damned good question, Maniah thought. The big ships could take care of themselves. And for now, the enemy seemed to be ignoring them. The

Arzucaldans were concentrating on the air base and the carriers, the most useful units if a war was starting. Without carriers to provide air cover the big battleships, despite their powerful armament and heavy armour, would hardly be more useful than an old river gunboat. Possibly less. A gunboat could, presumably, find a place to hide close inshore.

An enemy fighter flashed overhead, so close they could feel the shock wave as it passed. Must be out of ammunition, Maniah thought. Here we are, perfect targets on this dockside. He could have had us all.

In the distance she could see two officers hurrying toward her. One of them male, stocky, the other obviously female, with long brown hair falling about her shoulders instead of put up properly, as regulations demanded. Maniah was sure she recognised the unsteady gait, and as the pair drew closer the black patch where the woman's left eye had been confirmed it. Lieutenant K'Miwe Romiwero, *Warrior*'s electrical officer. Brilliant, but she had a tendency to drink a bit too much whenever she was off duty.

Soon the other had resolved himself into Commander (E) Ral L'Makim, the engineer officer. Maniah could still remember her surprise at finding him in her wardroom when she took command. She had last seen him in *Ro-1173*, the old training boat they had only half-jokingly referred to HIMS *Putrid*.

Back then she had been a young UnderLieutenant, only just out of the Imperial Naval College at Walkim, and going through the Submarine Branch's Officers' Basic Course at the Submarine School here at Koril Harbour. L'Makim had been a chief petty officer engineer in those days, running *Ro-1173*'s engine room. Those old *Ro* class boats didn't rate a commissioned engineer. She remembered him as a bit gruff, but really just an old softy at heart. And it had been very clear that he was a damn good engineer, and about as smart as they come.

The only thing that had surprised her about finding him in *Warrior*'s wardroom was the discovery that he had applied for a commission just after her class was graduated, and gave her the credit for nudging him in that direction. "Something you said about never letting yourself be satisfied with what you had if there was something more you could attain," he told her. "I decided that if I wanted to move up, get out of those old boats and into something modern, it was time for a commission. You get used to being the boss in the engine room, and in nuclear boats you have to be an officer to get that job."

He'd been commissioned two years later, but given his seniority and skills, the board had commissioned him as a full lieutenant, skipping underlieutenant entirely. His date of rank as commander was six months before hers, but as he was engineer branch that didn't matter. Only line officers could hold a command afloat. L'Makim could command a school, or a shipyard, but never a ship.

"I found Lieutenant Romiwero hanging upside down in her car just outside the main gate," L'Makim reported, in his gravelly bass voice.

The one-eyed electrical officer nodded. "It wasn't even a bomb," she complained. "Just some panicky bastard in a three-tonner. Rammed me broadside as I came around the corner and flipped my car right over."

"*Down!*"

A dive bomber flashed overhead, its two bombs dropping into the dock where *Harrier* lay exposed and damaged from the earlier attack. One of the bombs missed on the far side of the boat, exploding in the dock, where it still did considerable damage. The other smashed into the hull, blowing a great hole in the boat.

L'Makim looked over the edge of the dock and went ghostly pale. "We need to get the fuck away from here right now," he said. "That last one opened up the reactor vessel."

"There's no danger it will…" Ahno knew tactics, but had never been much of an engineer.

"Melt down? Blow up?" L'Makim shook his head. "No, there's no real danger of that. The reactor is shut down anyway. But there's going to be radiation leaking, so this particular area may not be all that healthy until we can get a decontamination crew in here to clean it up."

"Other end of the dock," Maniah ordered. "Everyone. Right now."

"I'll get on the phone to base engineering," L'Makim said, heading for the brow. "They'll want someone over here putting a temporary patch on that containment vessel." He pounded his fist on the brow railing. "Dammit, this is the *only* place those things are really vulnerable."

"The only place, ma'am?" a young sailor asked. "What's he mean?"

"He means," Romiwero said, "that at sea it is next to impossible to damage a reactor containment vessel. Even if you sink the boat, the things are strong enough to stay in one piece as deep as 14,000 metres."

"Which is deeper than anywhere in the ocean," Maniah added.

"A torpedo couldn't split it open?"

"It would have to get through the pressure hull first, and a torpedo would explode first. An armour-piercing bomb in dock is quite another matter."

The sailor nodded. He wasn't quite sure he understood, but at least the electrical officer had tried to explain. "Thank you, ma'am, I… *Here they come again!*"

The group scattered as an enemy fighter screamed over the dock, its guns blazing. Maniah found herself feeling very grateful for the tall gantries near either end of the dock. Their spidery structure complicated the Arzucaldan's approach.

A Navy half-ton truck screeched to a halt at the upper end of the dock and a frazzled looking civilian in an iridescent grey suit jumped down from the left-hand seat almost before it stopped. The driver immediately slammed the truck into gear and sped off as the civilian hurried up to the group at the brow.

He was a small, balding man, wearing thick spectacles which seemed to magnify his pale eyes grotesquely. Combined with his spasmodically work-ing jaw and thin lips they gave him the appearance of some sort of fantastic fish.

"Is one of you the captain?" he asked.

"I am," Maniah said. "I'm Commander Maniah."

"Mishtor Vaad," he said, by way of introduction, "base engineering. You're scheduled to be refloated tomorrow morning, correct?"

"Yes."

"Is everything closed up now? No hull openings that haven't been sealed?"

Maniah looked at L'Makim.

"Tight as a drum," the engineer said.

"So you could be refloated right now?"

"I suppose we could," L'Makim replied. "What good would it do?"

Vaad grimaced. "Possibly none. But the enemy seems to have gone away for the moment, in case you haven't noticed. Where would you prefer to be if he comes back? Sitting high and dry in dock? Or at sea, where you can submerge and hide?"

"Refloated or not, this boat isn't leaving harbour," Ahno said. "Most of the crew is still on leave."

"Could we put her on the bottom inside the harbour?" Maniah asked.

"You'd have to do it on batteries," L'Makim said. "The reactor's cold. Six hours at least to restart, and we can't do that until we're back in the water."

"Battery status?"

"I don't believe that's been checked yet this morning, but they should have a full charge. We've been running on shore power, so they should be topped up."

Maniah turned to the civilian. "How long to refloat her?"

"Normally, three to four hours. But I think we can get it down to under an hour. A bit rougher. Need to be handier with the lines to keep her cen-tred in the dock with the water coming in so much faster."

"Do it."

Vaad pulled out a key ring. "I'll get the valves unlocked. I could use a couple people to operate them. This old dock still has manual valves." He smiled. "You know, if the Arzucaldan's come back before we're done, you could always submerge in the dock. With any luck they'll think they've already sunk you and leave you alone."

"Armourer," Maniah snapped. "Take as many people as Mister Vaad needs and get those flood valves opened. Miss Romiwero, get your line han-dlers organised to keep the boat centred in the dock once she starts to come off the blocks."

She looked out over the devastated anchorage. Where there had been four big fleet carriers, now there were only three, and all three were sitting on the bottom of the harbour. *Emperor Felim* was the worst, partially capsized and resting on her port side. The other two had sunk on an even keel, and were sitting immobile, full of sea water, with their flight decks less than a metre above the oil-covered water.

The battleships and cruisers had fared better, but without the carriers to provide air cover they wouldn't be able to leave harbour, so it hardly mattered.

Looking toward the harbour entrance, Maniah could see five big attack subs heading out. The admiral would want them at sea before the enemy came back, both for their own safety, and to hunt down the Arzucaldan carriers.

But there should be seven, she thought. Had they lost two boats in the attack? Or was it just a matter of their crews still being on leave and they hadn't sufficient manpower to sail?

She turned to Ahno. "Rae, we need a crew. Do we have enough people to submerge? I don't care about leaving harbour, but do we have enough to man diving stations and put her on the bottom of the harbour out of the way?"

"No," he replied. "But I'll get on recruiting people to fill in. Maybe we can pull in some of the instructors from the Submarine School, or even some students. I think they have a cycle passing out this week. That lot should have learnt enough to be useful."

"Get on it."

She looked down into the dock. The water was starting to come in. Faster than normal, but it would still take time, and how much did they have?

Vaad had returned. "I've got the gate valves as wide open as they'll go," he said. He started. "Do you hear something? Jets?"

Yes, Maniah thought, there it was. Jet engines, a lot of them, and growing louder. Jets meant fighters, which wasn't necessarily such a bad thing. Fighters could carry bombs, but they couldn't carry big ones. And Arzucaldan torpedo and dive bombers, the planes that presented the biggest danger to the fleet, were all propeller driven.

She listened as the sound grew louder, turning to localise it, and as she did she began to relax. "They're coming from the northwest," she said.

Vaad looked at her curiously.

"That means they're probably ours. The enemy would be coming from the east, from the ocean."

A minute later her hope was confirmed as a flight of 18 Demon fighters—the Air Force version—swept overhead, heading out to sea. She had still seen no Navy fighters in the air, and she wondered if Rondor had survived the attack on the Fleet Air Base. She already presumed that the planes hadn't, or some of them would have been flying by now.

What were her parents thinking now? The attack would certainly have made the news by this time.

Warrior groaned. She wasn't quite afloat yet, but there was now enough water in the dock to start taking some of the pressure off the keel blocks. Vaad had said he could have the dock full in an hour. About half an hour had already passed. What would happen first, getting the boat fully afloat and out of the dock, or a second wave of attackers?

At least the Air Force was getting into it now. Presuming they didn't just get lost once they were out of sight of land. Demons were good fighters. Better than the Arzucaldan Sea Lightnings, or so her brother insisted. The Air Force versions were said to have a slight advantage over the Navy's, as they didn't have to stand up to carrier launches and landings, and being able to use lighter landing gear—without the need for a catapult shackle fitting—and eliminating the arrester hook saved several hundred kilos.

At the other side of the dock a work crew in full radiation gear was pouring concrete into *Harrier*'s reactor vessel. Full decontamination would take weeks, but this would at least stop any more radiation from leaking out. It would also destroy the reactor, making any repairs impossible, but the bomb had probably already done that.

"Give me a little more tension on that spring," Romiwero shouted.

There was definite movement now, Maniah thought.

A three tonner stopped at the head of the dock and eight chief petty officers climbed out of the back. A captain jumped down from the passenger's seat, slamming the cab door behind him, and started walking toward her, with the chiefs following.

Maniah saluted as he reached her. "Good morning, Captain Deponira," she said.

"Good morning, Captain," he replied, using her title rather than her rank. "We're your crew. Temporarily."

"Couldn't ask for better." Deponira was commanding officer of the Submarine School. The others were all instructors.

"Where do you want us?"

"Right here, for the moment. It looks as if the dock will be full in about a quarter hour. Once the gate's open, we'll see what happens.

But nothing did. The second wave never appeared, so instead of making use of her outrageously senior pickup crew to hide *Warrior* in the deepest part of Tufaria Bay, they carefully backed her out of the dock and moved her to the Armoury Pier to take on exercise torpedoes. She would proceed on her normal post overhaul schedule of trials, a day earlier than planned, but normal, nonetheless.

Two weeks would pass before *Warrior* was allowed to set out on her first war patrol.